TINSELED Up
in **TEXAS**

Halos & Horns: Book Five
A Christmas Novella

BY
LORI LEGER

Praise for "Tinseled Up in Texas"

"A second chance romance between a sexy Texas Marine and Nicki, a brave gal with a huge heart. This gem found a fantastic balance of sizzle and original plot, leaving this reader with visions of sugar plums and one delicious Marine dancing in her head. I dare anyone not to wish for a "Tex" of their own. Waiting for love and finding that perfect guy is what every gal dreams of. This warm little story delivers on all levels. Netflix or Harlequin definitely needs to bring Tinseled up in Texas to the silver screen; especially the last scene in the story."

Natasza Waters
Bestselling author (A Warrior's Challenge series)

ISBN-13: 978-1-940305-41-7

CAJUNFLAIR
PUBLISHING

P.O. Box 641
Kinder, LA. 70648
http://www.facebook.com/CajunflairPublishing
http://www.LoriLeger.com

Main character list and connection by series

La Fleur de Love Series
1) Some Day Somebody
   a. Carrie Jeansonne
   b. Sam Langley

2) Last First Kiss
   a. Giselle Granger (Co-worker of Carrie in Some Day Somebody
   b. Jackson Broussard (Co-worker of Carrie in Some Day Somebody)
   c. Scott "Red" McAllister (Carrie's cousin in SS and Jackson's friend)
   d. Dr. Tiffany LeBlanc (Jackson's doctor)
   e. Bill Broussard (Jackson's uncle

3) Brown Eyed Girl
   a. Dr. Tiffany LeBlanc (Jackson Broussard's surgeon in Last First Kiss)
   b. Red McAllister (Jackson's friend, Carrie's cousin Last First Kiss, SS)
   c. Tanner Collins (Tiffany's fiancé)
   d. Angelique Baptiste (Red's ex-girlfriend)
   e. Annie McAllister (Red's sister)
   f. Drake LeBlanc (Tiffany's brother)

4) Heaven in Your Eyes
   a. Annie McAllister (Red's sister in Brown Eyed Girl)
   b. Drake LeBlanc (Tiffany's brother in Brown Eyed Girl)

c. Vivienne McAllister (Annie & Red's mom, Brown Eyed Girl)

Halos & Horns Series
1) Green Eyed Temptation
    a. Angelique Baptiste (Red's ex-girlfriend in Brown Eyed Girl)
    b. Liam Nash (Annie M's. body guard in Heaven In Your Eyes)
    c. Det. Mike Harper (Brown Eyed Girl)
    d. Sarah Richard (abused woman with twin infants)

2) Sarah Smile
    a. Sarah Richard (Green Eyed Temptation)
    b. Tanner Collins (Tiffany's ex-fiance in Brown Eyed Girl)
    c. Mitchell Hebert (Sarah's brother)
    d. Daniel LeBlanc (Tiffany and Drake's father)

3) Meagan's Marine
    a. Meagan Hutton (Co-worker of Red McAllister, Heaven In Your Eyes)
    b. Mitchell Hebert (Sarah's brother, Sarah Smile)
    c. Niki Reeves (Sarah's friend)
    d. Matthew "Tex" Broussard (Mitchell's friend, US Marine)

4) One Year to Forever
    a. Haley Broussard (Tex's sister in Meagan's Marine)
    b. Lt. Cpl. Ben Bonin (Haley's boyfriend, US Marine sniper)

c. Niki Reeves (Meagan's friend in Meagan's Marine)

d. Tex Broussard (Mitchell's friend in Meagan's Marine)

e. Bo McAllister (Red's cousin)

5) Tinseled Up in Texas
   a. Matthew "Tex" Broussard (Best friend to Mitchell in Meagan's Marine)

   b. Nicole "Niki" Reeves (Meagan's friend in Meagan's Marine)

   c. Haley Broussard Bonin (Tex's sister in Meagan's Marine and One Year to Forever)

   d. Ben Bonin (Haley's new husband from One Year to Forever)

Prime Of Love Series
1) Running Out Of Rain
   a. Cynthia Robicheaux Ellender (Widow and old classmate of John Michael Ferguson)

   b. John Michael Ferguson (Zach's dad from Full Circle Love)

   c. Marilee Ferguson (John Michael's mom, married to J.D.)

   d. J.D. Ferguson (John Michael's dad, Marilee's husband)

   e. Bess Robicheaux (Cyn's mom)

2) Hanging On To Hope
   a. Allie Sarver (Cynthia's sister Running Out Of Rain)

   b. Clay Andrews (John Michael's

   c. Margie Andrews (Clay's ex-wife)

d. Jacques Bessette (Margie's fiancé)

3) Settling For More
   a. Sandra Campion (Wife of Marshall, mother to Ella, Maddie, and Brock)
   b. Marshall Campion (Sandra's husband, father of her children)
   c. Madison Campion (Mother to Isabelle, daughter of Sandra and Marshall)
   d. Ella Chandler (Kevin's wife, Maddie's sister)
   e. Kevin Chandler (Ella's husband, Maddie's old friend)
   f. Brock Campion (Ella and Maddie's brother, fiancé to Vonna Rose)
   g. Sharla Bowers (Brock's fiancée)
   h. Brennan McAllister (Red's cousin, Brown Eyed Girl, Bo McAllister's cousin in   One Year To Forever)
   i. Vonna Rose McAllister (Brennan's wife)

Other Books:
1) Full Circle Love (Four short stories in one book)
   a. Cathryn McDaniel
   b. Zachary Ferguson (son to John Michael Ferguson, grandson to JD in POL series)

2) Christmas 911 – Christmas Suspense novel by The Wild Rose Press
   a. Corinne Ritter
   b. Luke Oliver (Former sniper for US Marines)
   c. Tex Broussard (Cameo appearance – Meagan's Marine, One Year to Forever

DEDICATION

To Ms. Patsy and Mr. Ronald Sedtal ... I appreciate your support and I hope you don't mind me borrowing your names for purely fictitious purposes only.

Also, to any person who has ever had to put up with any kind of sexual harassment on the job or off of it, by any member of any gender—you don't have to take that. Not from anyone. This happens between opposite genders and same genders and is just as wrong in all situations. Be proactive. Believe in yourself. Believe in your right to speak out.

Finally, to any US Marine who has seen things that can't be unseen and lost members of his or her Marine family they'll never see again, you have my deepest appreciation. *"Ooh rah"* and God bless you all.

In closing, although I did address a couple of serious issues, this is a light hearted romance, with just enough heat to warm you up on a cold winter night. I enjoyed revisiting the Niki and Tex storyline and I'm glad I got this opportunity to give them some closure—I'd left them out in limbo long enough. I'm sure they'll continue to pop up in future volumes of my Halos & Horns series.

Prologue

February 25th

She should have known he'd show up looking like a poster boy for Man Whores of America.

Matthew "Tex" Broussard looked mighty fine in his best man attire—a supersized order of broad-shouldered sexy with a healthy side serving of testosterone. He'd paired a tailored black tuxedo jacket with a pressed white dress shirt, and tight-in-all-the-right-places black jeans. Tex removed his black felt Stetson upon entering the church, revealing a modified version of a military haircut, only with a bit more length on the sides and back. A becoming change from the longer length he'd worn the last time Niki had seen him—the neatly trimmed goatee he'd adopted since retiring from the Marines still adorned his handsome face, accentuating the masculine square jaw. His high quality black western boots were polished and shined, and a black bolo type tie with some type of silver medallion completed the look. The man had impeccable taste in clothing, down to the tiniest detail.

Nicole "Niki" Reeves couldn't say the same for his taste in company. He and his walking cliché of a 'date' entered the church—Tex's hand pressed intimately at the woman's completely bare backside down to barely concealed butt cleavage. As an extra insult, his "plus-one" faced Niki briefly, giving her a far too clear view of front cleavage pouring out of the skin-tight, leopard print dress. She'd accessorized the ensemble with spiked heels, flashy jewelry, and register-as-a-deadly-weapon grade fingernails. For some reason, Niki's mind flashed to a mental image, an often-seen memory of her Irish grandmother, twenty years dead now, making the sign of the cross while muttering a "Jaysus, Mary, and Joseph!"

Tex faced her then, nodded in her direction. "Nicole . . ."

Her name, coming from those lips—it always sent shivers down her spine. "Matthew . . ." she returned, sending him the slightest of nods. She shifted her gaze to the woman, whose over-applied makeup and false eyelashes had Niki wanting to attack her with a washcloth and a bar of soap. She reigned in the urge to scoff, or at least give the woman a single eyebrow-lift of disapproval, instead smiled politely before retreating into the room where the bride and her little boy were hidden away from curious gazes. In just minutes her best friend, Megan, would marry Mitchell Hebert, Tex's Marine brother. Mitch would be a great dad to Buck, Meagan's son from a previous relationship. As happy as she was for all three of them, this day couldn't end soon enough.

Once the ceremony began, Niki tried to concentrate as Meagan and Mitch exchanged their vows in the small church in Lake Coburn. She attempted to slow the pounding of her heart, no easy feat with Tex standing too damn close to her. Of course, she'd known Tex would be Mitchell's best man. The two former Marines had been friends for twenty years. No surprise there.

The truth was that even after all these months she hadn't been able to stop thinking about Tex, even though they'd only shared two nights of unbelievably hot sex. Niki shook her head, chastising herself for thinking such a thing in a church. At some point, she'd decided that whatever attraction they shared may be an underlying sign of something deeper, something worth pursuing. She'd devised a brilliant plan: pull him aside at some point during the private party for the bride and groom at Red's club and tell him that if he wanted to try again, she'd be willing.

She stood stiffly beside Tex, amazed at her own naiveté. In true Tex fashion—he'd arrived at the church with a woman who, judging from her attire and blatant stares at every male in the room, could very well be charging him an hourly rate. It amazed her that even after the infamous poll dancer incident years earlier, Tex still possessed such shock and awe capabilities. She cast a furtive glance at the six and half foot tall mountain of a man who exuded sex appeal, cringed when he caught her in the act. He gave her the classic one-sided, dimpled grin, his blue eyes sparkling with—what—amusement? Some twisted desire for revenge? Or did he possess some unfortunate need to flaunt his poor judgement in front of her? Damn him, anyway.

She squared her shoulders and faced the front of the church, making her final decision on the matter. She wouldn't waste another second thinking about the past, or a future, or anything else that concerned Tex Broussard.

* * * *

He hadn't expected Niki to come alone.

Tex had expected her to show up on the arm of some asshole with an MBA ready to discuss hedge fund strategies and investment opportunities. He'd debated with himself over whether or not to come alone, finally deciding to pad his own ego with a little preventative measure. He'd met "Star" last night at a new strip club in Beaumont. Like a last second impulse buy of beef jerky or gum at a cash register, he'd asked her to come along to the wedding as his 'plus one'. She hadn't needed much convincing, her only request being that she be allowed to use her stage name in hopes of drumming up a little business. A girl could never have a long enough list of clients.

The newlyweds had been less than enthusiastic once introductions were made. The "she's working her way through college" line had zero effect on his best friend's new bride. Meagan had simply shaken her head and walked away with a low grumble—one of those 'If you don't have anything nice to say, ignore the idiotic best man' moments. She *had* taken the time to toss one last "He's your friend—you deal with him," at her new husband. Mitch had given him a good reaming about it, telling him Niki had come solo—and rumor had it she'd wanted to speak to Tex about something.

Less than an hour into the reception, he made a lame excuse to Star and left to bring her back to Orange, a thirty-five-minute drive just over the Texas line. He dropped her off and exceeded several speed limits during the drive back to the reception. He made it back in under an hour, ready to throw himself at Niki's feet and beg forgiveness—only to discover she'd been called away for a family emergency. Her father had a stroke at her parents' home in St. Louis, Missouri.

He drove home that night, slightly depressed and more than a little disappointed at the turn of events. Just one more round of bad timing to ruin what might have been.

Chapter 1

Mid-November

One quick glance at the curvy blond behind the cash register called for a double-take. With her head lowered just for a few seconds he could have sworn she was someone else. All hope faded the instant she glanced his way.

"Yes sir, what can I help you with today?"

He tossed the bag of beef jerky on the counter along with a six-pack of Mexican beer, momentarily shocked at the "sir" tag she'd attached to him. She couldn't have been much older than twenty-one, and he was far from interested. Damn if it didn't sting anyway.

She studied his items, her pouty pink lips curving inward to hide a grin. "Looks like you're partying solo tonight."

He answered with a non-committal grunt, ready to go home and lubricate his wounded pride with a bottle of beer. She rang him up and he threw two bills on the counter. "Have a good day."

She smiled, baring perfect white teeth. "You betcha. Thanks. Come again."

He turned, shoved the door with his shoulder, managed to keep walking after she threw in one last comment.

"And come often, cowboy."

Tex approached his bright red, three-quarter ton Ford Diesel and climbed inside, the resulting tightness across his chest a strange mixture of pride and regret—strange for him, anyway. He looked at his reflection in the rearview mirror, gave himself a cocky grin. "At least you still got it." He started the truck to the rumble of four hundred and forty horses raring to go.

He thought of the other blond, the one whose image infiltrated his dreams occasionally despite his embarrassing best man display—what, nine months ago? Nicole 'Niki' Reeves—tall and lusciously curvy with gorgeous green eyes. She'd been on his mind lately, and he couldn't figure out why. Maybe his approaching birthday had given him a pitiful case of nostalgia about the one that got away. He groaned to himself, wondering how the hell he'd made it to forty-two. He'd had a couple of nights of fun with Nik, sure, as he had with lots of women before and since—but the memories of that lady had some definite staying power. Six years his junior, she'd be either thirty-four or thirty-five now depending on her birthday.

He'd swallowed his pride a month after the wedding and gone to her place in an attempt to explain his actions and ask for her forgiveness. That's when her roommate informed him she'd moved to St. Louis permanently in order to help her mom care for her father. One more round in the continuous pattern of suck-timing. He wondered if she still lived there. He'd made it a point never to discuss her with Mitch or Meagan when he spoke to them—his effort to avoid putting either of them on the spot. Did she have anyone special in her life? Mitch hadn't mentioned it, but then again, he wouldn't—not unless she'd married, or had a kid of her own—some kind of major milestone like that. All this time he'd figured no news was good news, meaning Nik was still single.

Tex backed out slowly, and then made his way to the parking lot's exit. He paused for passing traffic and reached for his phone to pull up Mitchell's number. Maybe the time had come to ask a few questions—one old jarhead to another. Tapping the button, he put the phone to his ear.

He caught his reflection in the mirror and shook his head at the tanned face, with his mom's eyes and his dad's dimples staring back at him. "Yeah, you still got it, dumbass. Too damn bad the only one you ever wanted doesn't want a damn thing to do with it."

* * * * *

The next day, around 9:00 a.m.

Nicole Reeves knocked on her best friend's front door and waited. Within seconds, it opened, revealing her ex-roomie's husband, former Marine, Mitchell Hebert. She pushed her sunglasses up onto her head and grinned. "Hey there—I was just in the neighborhood …"

His face lit up at the sight of her and he pulled the door open. "Nik! What the hell are you doing here? Meagan didn't say anything about you coming down for a visit."

She stepped into his open arms for a big bear hug. "I didn't tell her. I'm just passing through and wanted to stop in for a quick visit. Where is the harpy, anyway?"

His face fell. "This is one of those times when a phone call would have helped. She left early this morning to hit that big flea market a couple of towns over. She won't be back until late this afternoon. And I just dropped Buck off at a friend's house for an all-day birthday party."

She frowned. "You mean I'm stuck with you?"

His mouth twisted in a grin. "One little phone call would have prevented this. Come on in, anyway." He stepped aside to let her in and shut the door behind her. "What the hell brings you all the way to Monroe, Louisiana?"

Niki entered the coziness of the home, recognizing many of the photos and decorations from when she, Meg, and Buck had shared a three bedroom house back in Lake Coburn. A feeling of belonging seeped through her, making her long for days past. "I'm starting a new job in San Antonio next week. I just got the offer yesterday to replace someone who had to leave suddenly for health reasons. I needed a change so I said yes."

"So, you'll be working and living in Texas— who'd have thought . . ."

The smugness in his tone got her attention. "Spit it out, Marine. I've seen that look too many times and I know it means you're sitting on something." One side of his mouth lifted in that quirky, endearing grin of his. She loved the guy like a brother—a good thing, since he made her soul-sister so flipping happy—but his habit of knowing too much and sharing far too little irritated the living hell out of her. "Mitchell . . ."

He gave her a casual shrug. "You in Texas— San Antonio, at that—so close to a certain ranch in Blanco." He sucked in air through his teeth and cocked his head. "Sounds interesting, is all." He placed a hand on her shoulder and led her into the kitchen. "I just made a pot of coffee. Want a cup?"

"Do Texans love football? That's a big hell yeah, and I hope it's good and strong."

"Meg claims it'll eat through the silverware's plating."

"Perfect—I've been on the road since midnight, with a couple of breaks to stretch my legs and grab some grub." She lifted her nose and sniffed. "Do I smell brownies?"

He pointed to the table in the cozy breakfast nook. "Meagan's been up since before dawn. Said she couldn't sleep so she did some baking. Sit, I'll get you a couple of brownies and a cup of coffee."

"I've got to visit the little girls' room first. I'll be back." Minutes later, Niki stood before the sink washing her hands. She took the time to fluff her shoulder length hair and rub a little smeared eyeliner from the corner of one eye. She frowned, studying the lines of exhaustion on her face. "You're looking rough, Nik. Travelling does not suit you at all. Oh well . . ." She shrugged it off, knowing there wasn't a damn person that needed impressing in this house.

Niki headed back out to the kitchen, groaning at the sight of a full mug of coffee and a plate of brownies. She sat and crossed her legs before taking a cautious sip of the steaming liquid, rolled her eyes in pure bliss. "God, that's good. You're an angel." She bit into one chewy, chocolatey brownie, and nodded, recognizing her own recipe. "I taught Megs well."

"That you did." Mitch patted his belly. "I'm finding it harder to keep the belly at bay with all her good cooking."

"What a load of crap. Not about her cooking, of course. But that," she pointed to Mitchell's still-fit physique. "Is a far cry from 'dad bod'. I don't think you have anything to worry about." She sat back and gave him a silent perusal, waiting for him to share whatever was on his mind.

"You two must have some kind of mystical link."

"We *are* soul sisters—house mates for years— hell, our menses are still synchronized, even from two states away."

"That's—is that a thing?" Mitch frowned at her vigorous nod, eventually waving it off. "I find that disturbing as hell, but I'm talking about you and Tex."

Niki narrowed her gaze at the man sitting across from her. "Why would you say that?"

Mitch's grin turned smug. "He called me yesterday. We talked for a good while and he asked about you—more than once."

His revelation slammed her like a hurricane force gale. "Did he?" The cocky grin and tilt of Master Sergeant Mitchell Hebert's head made her want to wring his beefy neck. "Don't make me pull it out of you, Mitch. I'll tell Meagan you're holding back valuable intel and she'll cut you off for a week." She'd expected a bellow of laughter from the man Matthew "Tex" Broussard considered his best friend, as well as his Marine brother. She got a sad smile and a sober reply instead.

"He has regrets."

"Does he now? What happened? Did he get an STD from that stripper he brought to the wedding?"

"He brought her home early and by the time he got back you'd already received the phone call about your dad's stroke and hauled butt for Missouri."

Niki recalled the moment with horrifying clarity, as though it had occurred yesterday instead of back in February. It had signaled the beginning of the end of life as she'd known it. She sipped from her mug and set it on the table. "Your point being . . ."

He released his breath in a loud huff. "Maybe it's time to let that shit go, Nik. The man cares for you."

"*The man* has a funny way of showing it since he hasn't attempted to make the slightest contact with me since then."

"Maybe he was giving you time to cool off. Besides, he knew you had to move to Missouri to help your mom take care of your dad."

Her mom—Niki's breath hitched at the familiar stab of pain—it happened with every mention, image, memory, or thought of her mom. She loved her dad, but his stroke had prepared them—given them all time to say their goodbyes. Her mom's death, however, had come so suddenly, with no sign of illness, no warning—a massive aneurysm occurring in the middle of the night that had stolen her away from the daughter who adored her.

As painful as it had been to lose her so suddenly, Niki's mom would have wanted it that way. She'd said it often enough while caring so diligently for her husband. She had no desire to linger that way. She had also stated that after losing the only man she'd ever loved for forty years she couldn't stand being without him. Helen Reeves would insist that the God she loved had been merciful.

But Niki had to wonder at the wisdom and goodness of a God who would take both a girl's parents from her within two short months of each other. Waking up to find her mom gone that way had been the kind of nightmare she wouldn't wish on her worst enemy—the kind that left a gaping hole in her heart. No closure, no chance to say goodbye, and left only with the regret of not saying enough when she had the chance. The several weeks afterward had been so painful she'd taken the first offer from her company to transfer anywhere out of the city filled with such painful memories.

The great thing about working for such a large hotel chain was that she could find a job almost anywhere in the U.S. Her original goal had been to find a position in east Texas or southwest Louisiana to be closer to her friends. After her mom's death, her main objective had been to relocate anywhere away from St. Louis. If they'd offered a position in Maine, Seattle, or Florida—she'd have taken it.

She cocked her head slightly before posing her question. "Are y'all still set on moving back to Lake Coburn once Megs finishes pharmacy school at ULM?"

"That's the plan. I only have one sister and Meg and I would both like to be as close to Sarah and her family as possible. Sarah, Tanner and the twins aren't going anywhere. They're happy as clams down there."

Niki smiled at the thought of Sarah's adorable twin daughters. "How old are the girls now?"

"They're three-years-old and every bit as pretty as Sarah. Tanner insists he's locking them up as soon as they start showing an interest in boys."

"Of course *he'd* say that. Your brother-in-law was kind of a player before he met Sarah, wasn't he?" She laughed at Mitchell's eye roll.

"Player is probably an understatement. It terrified me when he started snooping around her. I'm ashamed to admit it now, but I did some interfering at the time that could have kept them apart. And that would have been a damn shame considering how he feels about Sarah and those little girls."

"It would serve him right to have guys chasing after *his* daughters, wouldn't it—even if they are only stepdaughters?" she said.

Mitchell glanced at the family portrait taken last Christmas of Sarah, Tanner, and the twins, Samantha and Danielle. "Maybe so, Nik. But if you ask any of them, there are no 'steps' in that family. Tanner Collins is the only daddy those girls have ever known—or remember knowing, thank God."

She nodded, recalling the stories of abuse Sarah had suffered at the hands of her first husband. Karma had prevailed, and they'd both gotten what they truly deserved in the end. Sarah's had come in the form of her second husband, a handsome surgeon who adored her and her two infant daughters—while her ex's had come from the dark and stormy waters of the Gulf of Mexico.

Mitchell leaned over the table and got eye to eye with her. "Don't think I don't know what you did there by changing the subject. I still say you need to give Tex a chance."

Niki bit her lower lip, wondered if she should tell him about her one attempt to do that. "I tried that once a couple of years ago. He wasn't home."

"What do you mean he wasn't home?"

"I called him first, to see if he wanted to go out sometime. I didn't know he'd moved to Blanco." She traced the rim of the coffee mug with one finger. "And later on I drove all the freaking way up there to that stupid ranch to talk to him, only he wasn't there."

"He never told me about that," Mitchell said.

"Because he doesn't know I went. It was a couple of Easter Sunday's ago. I drove for five and a half hours just to have some old couple tell me he'd gone to spend the day with his family." She groaned at the humiliating memory before releasing a frustrated breath, "See, that's karma telling us we're not supposed to happen."

"Yet . . ."

"Excuse me?"

"I don't know about karma or anything like that, but I'm thinking maybe that particular time wasn't right for either of you. Maybe your story with Tex isn't over yet."

She tilted her head and eyed him. "You have a right to think whatever you want, Mitch. I prefer to live in the real world if you don't mind."

Chapter 2

She stayed long enough to finish the cup of coffee and brownies before getting back on the road. Her boss had authorized a moving company to pack up her house and move everything to her new apartment in San Antonio by tomorrow. She wanted to get there first to check it out.

Niki reflected on Mitchell's revelation of Tex's phone call. Why would he ask about her now? She brushed it aside as another weird coincidence—one more nasty prank from a universe bound and determined to keep her eyeballs-deep in embarrassing moments and missed opportunities. She didn't have time to think about anything right now but getting her living arrangements and new job in order.

Niki maneuvered her vehicle directly through a line of rain and thunderstorms, the frontal system that promised much colder weather for the entire south. She pushed herself to keep driving, anxious to make it to her apartment before dark since this was her first trip into San Antonio. She made it a little after 5:00 p.m., barely early enough to check out her new surroundings.

Despite not knowing a soul in her new 'home', Niki liked what she saw. The realtor hired to find an apartment for her had certainly done her job well. The complex, nestled north of the city just off of U.S. 281 in Redland Ridge, was less than a ten minute drive to her company's corporate office. She parked in front of the manager's apartment and sent Meagan a text to let her know she'd made it safely, promising to call her once she made it into her new place. After a brief visit to the manager's office to submit proof of identity and have an official lease signing, she collected her keys and drove around to her new home.

Niki unlocked the front door and made a quick walk-through of the entire apartment. She brought in the few items she'd brought with her, plugging in her air bed to start the inflation process. She walked out to the covered back patio, phone in one hand and folding chair in the other. Within seconds, she was seated and waiting for Meagan to pick up. Her friend came out of the box swinging.

"I am so pissed at you, Niki! Why the hell didn't you tell me you were planning to stop by?"

Niki winced at her tone—knew she had it coming. "Honestly, Megs, it all happened so fast I didn't have time. I spent all of yesterday afternoon on the phone trying to get things ready on this end as well as making plans for my parents' place. I'm so exhausted, I guess I wasn't thinking."

"Mitch called me as soon as you left our house this morning, but I wanted to wait until I got home to call you. I made it in about five minutes ago."

"I know—I'm sorry. It was stupid not to call but I couldn't have stayed any longer than I did. Your hubby took care of me with a good cup of coffee. Those brownies were kick ass by the way."

"Uh huh," Meagan grunted. "So, you're in the apartment already?"

"I am, with only the bare essentials." She left her chair long enough to check on the progress of her air bed and went back out to the patio. "It's a nice place. Only a one bedroom but the living area is as roomy as our old house in Lake Coburn." She stared out at the tiny plot of lawn opposite the patio, wondering if she'd have to mow it. It hit her suddenly—how alone she was. Her throat clogged with an unexpected urge to cry. "Megs . . ."

"What? What's wrong?"

Niki blinked back tears as she stared outside. The long shadows of the early fall dusk had turned to darkness quickly thanks to the recent end of daylight savings time. Nighttime only intensified her loneliness. "I'm—I feel like—oh God, what have I done? Ever since mom died I've wanted to get out of St. Louis. I couldn't wait to get away—to escape from everything. And now I'm here and I'm thinking, what the hell have I done?" She choked on a sob. "I'm all alone here, Megs. I don't know a single other person in this city. Why did I do such a stupid thing?"

"Did you give Mitchell your address? The apartment number too?"

She sniffed. "Yes. Why? Are you planning to come for a visit already?"

"I wish I could, hon. But my class schedule won't allow it. I took a rare day off of studying today to look for a few pieces of furniture for Buck's room. I'll make it over there one day, but until then, describe your place to me. What's it like?"

Niki wiped her eyes and stepped inside, a little chilly now that the cool dry air had circulated throughout the apartment. "Paint job is fresh—the whole place has this rustic Texas vibe to it."

"What's the kitchen like?"

"Tiny, galley style but the stainless steel appliances are new. It's nice, but really small."

"I guess you'd have had to spend more to get units with a gourmet kitchen."

"Nope, every unit has the exact same kitchen layout. I'm guessing it's not a priority here. People must eat out a lot—lord knows I saw enough restaurants and fast food joints on the way here." She walked from room to room, describing the other areas to Meagan.

"Got any idea how you plan to decorate the place?"

"Not the slightest." Niki stopped in the middle of the living area and looked around. "Although . . ." She went to one suitcase, pulled out a handful of framed photos and positioned each photo on the quartz countertop. One of her with her parents, a group shot of Meagan, Mitch and Buck, flanked by Tex on one side and herself on the other, taken the day of Meagan and Mitchell's wedding, and another shot of herself with Meagan and Buck.

"That's better," she said, releasing a small satisfied sigh, immediately comforted by the familiarity.

"Hey, Nik?"

"Yeah?"

"Have you eaten supper yet?"

"No, and I'm starving. I'm too tired to drive anywhere tonight, so I'll either have to order delivery or eat some of the snack food I brought along."

"Don't do anything. Mitch and I have taken care of that for you tonight."

"What do you mean?"

"I mean expect a delivery. You've got about five minutes to make yourself presentable."

"I drove seventeen hours today, Megs. I'm too tired to make the effort to impress anyone tonight." Regardless of her words, she headed to the small bathroom and stood in front of her mirror. She put her phone on speaker and dug through her bag to find a few essentials. No use making a bad first impression on a young delivery kid working his or her way through college. "What kind of delivery?" The sound of her voice bounced off the bare tiles. She could surely go for a meat lover's pizza with extra cheese.

"You're fixing your make-up right now, aren't you?" Meagan said, sounding slightly amused.

"Am not!" Niki stuck her tongue out at the phone, thankful they weren't face timing. She dabbed a bit of foundation on her T-zone and under her eyes, before applying a bit of lip color. A quick fluff of hair flattened by hours of running her hands though it had her reaching for a can of hair spray.

"I hear hair spray." Meagan's laughter echoed from the phone's speaker against the bare walls.

"Shut up, harpy. I told you, I'm hungry. No sense in scaring away the wet-behind-the-ears delivery kid. Who knows, maybe he's a lineman for the local university's football team. I could be a *cougar*."

Meagan's snicker of laughter carried to her. "Or a water boy for the high school football team and you could be charged as a pedophile."

"Ugh! Why must you rain on my parade?" Niki swiveled at the knock on the front door. "Oh, I think the food's here." Her stomach rumbled in anticipation as she approached the door.

"I'll let you go so you can enjoy your delivery. Oh, and Nik?"

Niki reached for the door knob and paused. "Yeah?"

"You can thank us later."

Niki stared at the call ended icon on the screen before slipping the phone into her back pocket. She pulled open the door and stared at the massive figure blocking the doorway. A black Stetson shadowed the crystal blue of his eyes, but it couldn't hide the outline of those pecs, clearly defined through his long sleeved T-shirt—or the tree-trunk forearms attached to broad shoulders— not to mention those damned irresistible dimples.

One hand reached up to touch the brim of his hat. The other held out a large bag bearing the name of a Mexican restaurant. "Special delivery."

And that *voice*—that sexy as sin bass that had the power to turn her insides to a quivering mass of mush.

Oh. My. God. Somehow, she managed to harness those three words, keep them from bursting forth in an astonished blast of sound. She took one deep breath, then another before releasing it slowly to respond with a performance that should surely earn her some kind of award from those snoots in Hollywood. "Hi, Tex." She placed a hand on her stomach, hoping to calm her nerves.

"Hey, Nik. How you doing?"

Had those peepers turned a deeper shade of blue in the several months since she'd last seen him? Were those shoulders even broader than before? "What—what are you doing here?" He flashed the grin she'd always found so irresistible. Trouble was, so did plenty of other women. That thought sobered her as well as any cold shower.

"We didn't want you to move in to your new place without seeing at least one friendly face."

"We—Mitchell called you and set this up?"

He tilted his head slightly. "Don't go getting all pissed at them for not wanting you to feel so alone in a new city, Nik. If we can't be anything else, I'd like us to be friends." He removed his hat and dipped low to get eye level with her. "Do you think that's possible?"

She stared at him, winced when her stomach growled at the delicious aromas coming from the bag. His laughter rumbled like an outboard motor in the vacant room. She gave in to her hunger pangs and stepped aside to wave him in. "Sure, Tex. I can always use a friend in this city, especially one who brings me food. Get in here, you big redneck. I'm famished."

He walked in and nodded as he looked around. His gaze fell on the three framed photos and he leaned forward to study them closer. "I love what you've done with the place so far."

She shrugged. "I needed something familiar to get me through the night until the rest of my stuff gets here." She waved a hand at her empty room. "Sorry I can't offer you a place to sit—oh, wait—I have a chair." She brought the folding chair in from the patio and set it before him. "Have a seat."

He shook his head. "My mama didn't raise me to sit while a lady stands."

She gave him a half-hearted eye roll. "Spare me. Besides, I'll sit up here on the counter." She backed up to the kitchen peninsula and attempted to lift herself. She slipped once and froze when he approached and placed the bags onto the surface.

With a tilt of his head, he extended both hands toward her and paused. "May I?"

She quirked one brow, deciding it wouldn't hurt to let him help her. He placed his huge hands on each side of her waist and lifted her easily onto the counter. "Thanks." She adjusted her position, trying to ignore the tingle created by his touch. She averted her gaze, hoping to avoid the impending blush.

He stepped aside and opened the first bag. "I remembered you like Mexican food, and particularly loaded chicken quesadillas. I ordered the house special with extra guacamole for you." He lifted out one foam container and opened it for her.

She lifted the plate to her face and breathed in. "This smells delicious. What'd you get?"

"The burrito supreme plate with an extra chimichanga—and an order of chips and salsa we can share. This place has the best damn salsa I've ever tasted." He lifted out a second plate and opened it, tearing off the lid to use as a container for the tortilla chips.

Niki kicked off her slip on shoes and pulled one foot up under her. She balanced the plate on her leg and dug into her food. She closed her eyes, savoring the delectable combination of flavors, and managed to speak after swallowing the first bite. "Oh m'gosh, this is so freaking good!"

Standing beside her, he gave a satisfied grunt until he finished his own first mouthful of food. "I'm glad you like it. Did I hear Mitch right when he said you'd been on the road since midnight or something?"

She nodded. "I wanted to get here before my stuff arrives tomorrow. The manager told me over the phone it was move-in ready but her idea and mine of ready may not have jived. I wanted to come check it out for myself." She looked around. "But this place is great. It seems to be a nice area."

Tex ducked his head to look out the front windows. "You should be safe enough here. But if you're ever worried about going somewhere alone, just give me a call. I'll be glad to show you around, or be your escort—" He faced her, leveling his gaze on her. "I mean it, Nik—anytime, day or night. If you need me, just call and I'll be here, or there, or anywhere you need me."

She tore her gaze from his eyes to settle on his lips—anything to avoid the message being sent out in waves. The man oozed irresistible, 'good ol' southern boy' sex appeal, wrapped up in six foot and five inches of brawn, all tanned and bronzed from working in the hot Texas sun. Good grief, but she'd had it bad for this cowboy once. She couldn't afford to fall for it—not again. She needed to keep her wits about her—stop letting her girl parts influence the decisions her mind should be tending to. One corner of his mouth tipped up in a sexy semi-grin that had her sucking in her breath. She jutted her chin toward the chair. "Sit. Now."

"Yes, ma'am." He sat obediently, balancing his plate in one hand.

"How's your place in Blanco?"

His head bobbed and he smiled. "It's good. Quiet, peaceful—it's what I needed for a while."

She frowned. "And now?"

"I still want it. I just don't need it."

"I get that."

His gaze locked on hers again. "You do?"

"Sure, there's a huge difference between wanting something and needing it. And whether or not you get that something can make a difference in your life—for good or bad." Tex stared out her window again, looking far too pensive for a cowboy out for a good time. She grabbed her phone, deciding they needed a little background music in the room. She started the upbeat country playlist that had accompanied her from St. Louis all the way to San Antonio, and then turned her attention back to her food.

"So what is it *you* need, Niki? What made you leave Missouri to come all the way here?"

She blinked several times, put her plate off to the side and wiped her hands on a paper napkin she'd pulled from the bag. "I had to get away from there. My parents . . ." Her voice faltered, but she managed to finish. "My parents are both gone now and being in that house, with all those memories and neither of them around anymore." She shook her head in several quick, jerky movements. "I just couldn't stay another day. So I begged my boss for a transfer."

"Why Texas? Why here?"

She laughed, suspecting he wanted to hear she'd chosen this place because of its close proximity to a certain ex-Marine—*him*. "I've been chomping at the bit to get out of there for two months, Tex. And someone had to almost die to open up a position. It's literally the first opening they had at the corporate level."

"Oh, the corporate level," he said, grinning. "Excuse the hell out of me."

She fought the urge to reach out and run her fingers through his light brown hair highlighted with natural blond streaks. He kept it slightly longer than when she'd last seen him at the wedding. Tex's smile slowly dissolved from his face and she braced herself for the well-meaning words sure to come. *Time heals everything ... they're in a better place ... there's a reason for everything ... she'd want it this way . . .* All true, but not extremely helpful to the person struggling to put one foot in front of the other after losing her entire family.

"I'm sorry about your parents, Nik." He lifted one hand and let it fall. "Mine are both still alive so I don't have the slightest idea what to tell you. It sucks like hell that you lost them the way you did." He looked down at his food and shook his head. "All I can say is that if you start to feel low I can be here in under an hour. Give me a call—if you want to talk, go for a drive, take in a movie, or need a shoulder to cry on—whatever. I'm here for you."

She swallowed, stunned by his honest sincerity, and somehow managed to spit out a whisper soft "Thank you."

He reached out to place a hand on her ankle. "I'm serious, Nik. That's some heavy shit to carry around and your *friends* don't want you thinking you have to carry it all alone."

Niki heard her old roommate in every word of that little speech—big time. "Megs told you to say that, didn't she?"

Tex gave her a cheesy grin. "See, I told her you'd know that didn't come from me, but that doesn't stop me from meaning every word of it. I'm serious about that. If you need me, I'll drop whatever I'm doing to come over."

She grinned, unable to stop the next words from coming from her mouth. "Whatever you're doing—or *whomever* you're doing?"

He clicked his front teeth together and sucked in his breath. "Ouch—okay, I guess I had that coming to me."

"You really did. But, that's it from here on out. After this act of tremendous kindness, we're even. I'm letting all of that go, I promise."

He stared at his plate and cocked his head to face her. "It'd sure be cool if you did."

She raised her right hand. "No more pole-dancer jabs, I promise."

"Good."

"Or stripper jokes."

"Nicole . . ."

Her laughter rang out between them. "I'm just jerking your chain, Tex."

He picked up his plastic fork. "I'm gonna finish eating now. I suggest you do the same before it gets cold."

They finished their meals, making small talk between songs on her phone's playlist. Tex stood, as though readying himself to leave. The room seemed to close in on Niki as a full-blown case of panic set in. "Wait, Tex. Tell me more about your ranch!"

* * * *

Tex paused at the hitch in her voice, stared into the huge green eyes that had captivated him from the moment he'd first walked in and seen her again. Her full red lips quivered as she tried to hold it together. He wasn't as dense as some people thought—he recognized the sound of desperation when he heard it. It's not that she wanted *him* to stay—she just didn't want to be alone. He'd play along—stick around for some small talk. "It's not my ranch. It's been in the owner's family for generations, as most ranches are. I came close to buying it outright—had actually moved there thinking I would, but the family decided to hang on to it a few more years. I believe one of their grandsons is beginning to show interest in running it one day."

"Why were they considering selling it?"

"The only one of the Sedtal's kids interested in running the place was killed in Afghanistan." He lowered his head, remembering the day Bobby's number had come up. "Bobby Sedtal was a damn fine Marine, and a good friend. Bobby, Mitch, and

I—man we'd been through thick and thin together. He had a plan—twenty years in the Corps, then retire and take over the ranch. It didn't happen, of course."

"I'm sorry, Tex."

He wiped his hand roughly over his eyes and face. "Anyway, nobody else in the family had the heart to take on the responsibility of running the place. Mitch and I would come and visit his folks from time to time and I always loved it up here. When the ranch fell on hard times, I had a good chunk of money saved up and convinced his dad, Mr. Ron, to sell me the section with an old rundown cabin, access to the lake for fishing, and the one mile strip of land with a road leading to the place. It gave me a place to call home and got them out of a bind."

"So you live in the cabin alone?"

"Yeah. It's not rundown anymore, either. I've worked on it and brought it into the twenty-first century."

She smiled. "I've got this image of a primitive cabin running through my mind."

He laughed. "I guess some people might still consider it primitive, but I call it home."

"So, you work as a hand on the ranch?"

"I'm glad to help out around the place when they need me but he's got a good foreman and crew to do the lion's share of the work. I bought my truck and this place outright with my savings. My retirement keeps me in grub and supplies for home improvements and taking care of my horse."

He slipped his thumb into his back pocket. "I'm not sure if this is a permanent thing or not. I know my mom was kind of disappointed when I moved here after being away from home so long. Once Meagan finishes school, and she, Buck, and Mitch move back down to Lake Coburn, I was thinking of finding something closer to home—somewhere between Lake Coburn and my folks place." He shrugged one shoulder. "Until then, this place works for me."

"So, they pay you to work the ranch?"

"Nah, I don't ask for anything. I just love staying busy and helping them out when I can."

"Do they have many cows on the farm?"

He gave her a disgusted snort. "It's a cattle ranch, not a cow farm."

"Is that a Texas thing?"

He frowned. "It's a ranch thing. No respectable rancher in the U.S. of A. would ever call him or herself a cow or cattle farmer. They do have ranchers who also grow farm crops, either to feed their own stock or to market for a profit. Ranchers have to diversify these days or they won't survive."

"Are there female ranchers around here?"

"Sure there are. You being the modern woman you are, I'd have thought you'd expect that."

"I guess … it's just that when I think of cattle ranchers, I think of the old westerns my dad used to watch."

"Didn't he ever watch *The Big Valley*?"

"I don't know. Why?"

"Barbara Stanwyck played Victoria Barkley and ran her dead husband's ranch along with their four adult children."

Her face remained blank until her mouth opened. "Wait—was one of the sons married to Farrah Fawcett at one time?"

"That would be Lee Majors who played Heath, the illegitimate son of the dead husband. Give the lady a prize!" he called out in a carnival barker imitation.

She nodded thoughtfully. "Yeah, my dad watched that. That guy was hot when he was young."

"So was his sister, Audra, but the point I'm trying to make is that there *are* female ranchers. So, give me the grand tour of your new digs." He placed his hands around her waist and helped her off the cabinet.

She pulled down her T-shirt and extended one arm. "You've seen the kitchen and dining room with its cute little bay window. This door leads to the patio area." She walked a few feet further into a larger open area. "Here we have the very spacious living room—at least it is with no furniture. There's a tiny little office area over here with a built-in desk right next to the foyer. Here's the bathroom." She entered the bathroom through a door on one end and into the bedroom through a second on the opposite end. "And here is the only bedroom."

He pointed to the fully inflated air mattress. "You've thought of everything. At least you won't have to sleep on the floor tonight."

"An airbed is essential." She waved her arm at the bare room. "You're looking at the extent of this girl's idea of 'roughing it'."

He nodded, keeping all thoughts of what he'd like to do with her on that airbed to himself. "When the moving company gets here with your furniture tomorrow, give me a call. I'll be glad to come over and help you get this place in order."

She raised her face to him, her eyes wide. "Tex, are you sure? I could use the help but I know you must have things to do. You already took time out of your day to drive all the way over here just to bring me supper."

He pulled on his goatee, debating whether she needed to hear the truth. "Honestly? When Mitch called me, I was already in the city."

"Oh . . ." She seemed to deflate before his eyes. "Y-you weren't on a date, were you?"

"No. I was doing some shopping." Did he really want her to know he'd ached for some kind of human contact? That the solitude of living alone sometimes became downright unbearable? "Not that I wouldn't have driven here tonight—but by coincidence, I didn't have to."

"Okay, then. If you don't mind driving back here tomorrow, I'd surely appreciate the help. I could even pay you—"

He raised his hand to cut her off. "*Don't*—that's an insult, Nik. Give me a call as soon as the moving van shows up. We'll have you settled in here in a jiffy." He pulled out his phone. "I don't know if you have my number. I had to get a new plan since we last spoke and it was entirely too much hassle to port the old number." They spent a few minutes updating contact information and he slipped his phone in his shirt pocket. "Now, I really should get back before Captain Perry sends out a search party." He loved the way her brow furrowed, obviously stumped by his comment. "He's my stallion. If I don't pay him his evening visit tonight I'll pay for it tomorrow."

Her head cocked adorably to one side. "What'll he do? Kick you or something?"

"No, but he'll ignore the hell out of me." He shook his head. "It's the damnedest thing. He literally turns his back on me, shifts his entire hind end around and refuses to look me in the eye. Takes him a day or two to get over it."

The room filled with her sudden burst of laughter. "I've never heard of such a thing. I had no idea horses could be that temperamental."

"Oh lady, you have no idea. I've had Cap for several years. My pop trained and raced him for me while I was in the Corps. He's fast, extremely virile, and brings in some damn good stud fees. But when I first retired, I bought a beautiful Palomino mare named Nina. She used to nip at any female within arm's reach of me."

Niki's face lit up. "Seriously? That must have caused quite a problem for a stud like you."

Heat infused his face until he sent her a sheepish grin. "I finally brought her back to the original owner. I couldn't risk the backlash of getting sued by some woman."

"Did you still have her when we first met?" she asked.

"Yeah . . ." He looked at his boots. "It's a good thing you never made her acquaintance. She probably would have taken a good chunk out of you."

She cocked her head. "Instead of a nip? Why's that?"

He shrugged. "She probably would've, that's all." How did he answer that? The simple fact was that Nina's nips grew in proportion to Tex's attraction to his female companion. Somehow, that horse sensed it. And he'd never been as attracted to any woman more than he had Nicole Reeves—not before nor since their first meeting.

She nodded and took a couple of steps toward him. "You need to be on your way. Thanks again for supper, Tex. And if you feel like coming tomorrow, I'd appreciate the help."

"It's good to have you in the neighborhood, Nik." He extended his arms and she walked into his embrace. He hugged her tightly, maybe longer than he should have. But damn it felt good. And not just in the hottest-sex-he'd-ever-had way, either—although the night they'd accidentally been locked inside Red's club had certainly hit an all-time high for him. But in a way that warmed him—starting in his heart and spreading to encompass his entire chest and torso. She reminded him of home, of belonging—had him wondering what his mom and pop would think of her. Eventually, he let her go, clearing his throat as he stepped away. "I'll see you tomorrow, Nik."

She walked him to the door, blinked several times, as though trying not to cry. It nearly killed him when she crossed her arms tightly against her chest and bit down on her trembling lower lip.

He paused and leaned over to get eye level with her. "Hey, listen—if you don't want to stay here in this empty apartment tonight, you are more than welcome to stay the night at my place. It's a one bedroom cabin, but I do have furniture, a well-stocked fridge and pantry, and a big comfy couch you can crash on. Or we can deflate that air bed of yours and bring it along." He raised both hands. "No strings attached." She looked around her empty apartment, and for a moment he thought she'd cave.

Straightening her shoulders, she lifted her chin and shook her head. "Thanks, and I appreciate the offer, Tex. But I think it's time to pull up my big girl panties and do this. I'll be fine."

He nodded, admiring her determination. "Alright then, you have a good night, Nicole."

"You too, Tex."

"He lifted his phone from his shirt pocket and waved it at her. "Call me."

She graced him with a smile that sent a sparkle to her beautiful green eyes. "I will, and thanks again."

He spent the drive back to his cabin replaying every moment he'd ever spent in her presence, from the night of the Halloween party at Red's club nearly three years ago, until now. They had only spent two evenings together but he'd spent many more lusting after her anytime she was near. Once their best friends became a couple, they saw each other frequently. His last sighting of her at Meagan and Mitchell's wedding marked the final in a long line of missteps with that lady.

Tex pulled up at his cabin and headed straight for Cap's stable. The big guy gave him several impatient whinnies, swinging his huge head back and forth, as though chastising him for being late.

"I know, I know! Sorry Cap, but I couldn't leave a lady in distress, could I? I'm sure you can relate to that." He poured a scoop of sweet oats into his horse's feed bucket and filled his trough with fresh water. He spent a little more time brushing Cap's coat than normal before leaving him to enter the solitude of his cabin.

Tex showered, made the mistake of recalling his and Nicole's last encounter, and found himself so hard he had to finish with a shockingly cold shower. Afterward, he stretched out on his sofa, wishing like hell Nik had taken him up on his offer to spend the night with him in his cabin.

He closed his eyes, imagining her as she looked before he'd walked away tonight. Damn it all— tomorrow couldn't get here soon enough.

Chapter 3

Niki stood in the center of her new apartment and stared at the results of all her and Tex's hard work. The truck had arrived at 8:00 a.m. this morning and after sending off a text to her 'neighbor' thirty miles to the north, he'd arrived forty minutes later, armed with breakfast, coffee, and the strength of three men. Within two hours, Tex had reassembled her bed and placed all the furniture where she wanted it. By noon, they'd emptied all the boxes and loaded them into the back of his truck for disposal.

He approached her and crossed his muscled arms across his chest. "It's looking good, Nik. I think you'll be very comfortable here."

She nodded, already feeling more at home surrounded by her own things. "I can't believe we're nearly finished." She swiveled her head to look up at him and smiled. "This would have taken me two days working alone. I owe you big for this." The old Tex would have flexed his arms and made some smart-ass remark about what she could do to repay him. This Tex just smiled and waved off her comment.

"You don't owe me a thing. I told you, I'm here for you as a friend. And this is what friends do for each other, right?"

She smiled, accepting his comeback. "They also do nice things in return for each other. How about I return the favor with a home-cooked meal, Mr. Broussard?"

His head cocked slightly to one side. "I knew you baked but I didn't think you liked to cook."

"Are you kidding? I love to cook." She pointed to her new kitchen. "Nothing says 'home' like breaking in that brand new stainless steel range."

"You're probably exhausted," he said, looking doubtful. "Why don't you let me take you out to eat instead?"

She raised both hands to her ponytail, removing and replacing the band for the twentieth time that day. She'd passed on applying make-up that morning, deciding she didn't want to look like she was trying to impress him, especially when faced with hours of manual labor. "But then I'd have to make myself look presentable. Besides, this way I can scope out the best grocery stores around here." She tilted her head to search his gaze. "Got any suggestions?"

"I'd have to be crazy to pass up home cooking, so if you want to cook, I'd appreciate it. There's a locally owned chain store right around the corner. I usually find whatever I need there."

They were back in an hour and putting the last of Niki's groceries away. She made him sit at the kitchen island while she prepared and stuffed two chicken breasts. Once everything was in the oven she handed Tex a fresh bottle of beer and they moved to the living room. She curled up on one end of the overstuffed couch she'd brought from her parents' home with a bottle of water. "How's the family? Is Haley still seeing that Marine?"

Tex smiled at the mention of his baby sister. "Ben's not active anymore, but I guess you could say that. They were married a few months ago."

"I hadn't heard—that's good to know they're still together."

"Yeah, they're stupid happy, you know? I've never seen two people so into each other and so sure about what they want out of life. They both finished school and have started their careers. Last I heard they're looking into buying a home."

"And your parents?"

"Still crazy about each other and keeping busy. I haven't seen them in a while. I'll be going there for Thanksgiving next week though."

"Thanksgiving . . ." She hadn't even thought about the holidays. Now that she did, she dreaded them.

"Do you have any plans?"

"I haven't even thought about it." She'd cringed at the early onslaught of Christmas advertising on TV—switched channels if she could get to it fast enough. "I—I guess I've tried not to think about it."

"Shit." He wiped his hand over his goatee and sent her the sympathetic look she'd seen so much of the last few months. "I'm sorry, Nik. It's your first holidays without your parents."

She blinked several times hoping to keep the flood of emotions from pouring forth. "It's just that my mom—she loved the holidays. Did them up right, you know?" She wiped tears from the corners of both eyes. "She especially loved Christmas … didn't stop decorating until she'd covered every inch of the house."

He crossed one foot over his knee and gave her a sympathetic smile, revealing a single dimple. "Let me guess, multiple trees?"

Niki swallowed the lump in her throat. "No less than three." She smiled back at him through tears. "I remember a few years when every room in the house had trees."

He chuckled. "I'm trying to imagine them in the bathrooms."

"They were tiny tabletop trees in the two bathrooms, but they were trees." She pointed to the door leading to the patio. "You saw them. All of those large green plastic boxes you stacked in that storage building for me? Those are all filled with Christmas decorations. I suppose I'll have to pick and choose. This place isn't nearly big enough to hold all of those decorations, but I wouldn't know how to choose. Part of it on display without all of it being on display—I don't know. It wouldn't feel right. And I could never get rid of anything. Mom . . ." Niki lowered her head. "Mom went crazy decorating the house last Christmas, too. Sometimes I wonder if she knew, Tex. I remember my trip home so well. I walked through the door and my senses were immediately overwhelmed. I stood there, taking in all the smells—from the real tree in the living room, to the cinnamon apple candles she had burning all over the house, to the cookies baking in the oven."

Niki closed her eyes, letting the memory wash over her. "And the entire house awash in red, green, and gold decorations, and dripping with tinsel." She laughed and shook her head. "That woman adored her tinsel, no matter how many times I told her I thought it was tacky. She said a tree wasn't a tree without it—red, gold, green, or silver—but *never* blue. Mom can't stand the color blue in any Christmas decorations. I mean she *couldn't* stand it . . ."

* * * *

Her smiled faded, and it hit him then—how alone this poor lady must be feeling right now. How completely adrift from everything she'd ever known. With both parents gone, she had no place to call home anymore, no anchor, and no place to go. He could help her with that, if she'd let him.

"You're coming with me to my folks' house for Thanksgiving."

She blinked once and faced him. "Tex, no … you don't have to feel sorry for me."

He raised his hand. "I won't hear another word about it. My mom and dad would love to have you."

Her eyes brightened just a little. "Will Haley and Ben be there?"

"Absolutely—at least for part of the day, anyway. They may have to make the rounds at his family's place in Lake Coburn. Haley will be excited to see you."

"Then I accept, but only if I can contribute to the menu. Find out what I can bring."

He pulled his phone from his pocket. "I'll do you one better and let you ask her yourself." He raised one hand at the look of panic on her face. "Relax. Mom's a good cook but she's not much of a baker. If you offer to bring a dessert she'll be thrilled." Tex walked to the back door for better reception before making the call. He explained the situation to his mom, hoping she didn't have a problem with it.

Angie Broussard waited until he'd finished before speaking. "Matthew, are you asking to bring a date to our Thanksgiving dinner?"

He stared at Niki, still seated on the couch, and still looking alone in a world too big for her. "She's a friend, Mom."

"Look son, you know I love you, but it could get tricky trying to figure out what to say to a stripper or a pole dancer."

Tex stepped out onto the patio and wiped his free hand down his face. "Well damn, I guess I have that coming to me, too, but it's not like that at all. As a matter of fact, Haley knows Niki."

"Haley's right here. Let me ask her if she knows someone named Niki."

"Niki Reeves," he said, waiting for his mom to relay the message to his sister. His sister's whoop of excitement had him grinning.

"Oh my God! He's seeing Niki again? Let me talk to him." Tex waited through some shuffling on the opposite end of the connection, had to pull the phone from his ear at his sister's delighted squeal. "You're bringing Niki here for Thanksgiving?"

"Yes, unless you scare her off. It's a friendly invitation."

The phone exploded with her laughter. "If you didn't scare her off with your caveman antics when you first met, nothing will. I can't wait to see her again."

"She wants to talk to mom—see what she can contribute to the meal."

"Okay, but listen up, big brother. If you've got another chance with this girl, don't you dare screw it up. I want her as a sister-in-law, do you hear me?"

"I hear you, squirt. Now put Mom on the phone, will you?"

Tex stood watching and listening as Niki introduced herself to his mom over the phone and settled on what she could bring to the Thanksgiving meal. Her face lit up when Haley hi-jacked the phone from his mom again. Niki spent a couple of minutes catching up with his little sister before handing the phone back to him, obviously appeased for the moment.

"Here you go. I think your Mom wants to speak to you again."

He put the phone to his chest. "Did you get everything straightened out?"

Niki's face stretched wide with a smile. "I'm baking the pies."

"Okay." He put the phone to his ear. "Mom?"

"Hey, son. Your sister says to tell you if you screw this up she'll castrate you herself. Apparently she thinks Niki Reeves is exactly the kind of woman you need in your life."

Tex watched as Niki peeked in the oven to check on their meal. No make-up, hair pulled back in a ponytail and probably exhausted, she was still the sexiest and most beautiful woman he'd ever known. The last two days spent in her company had shown him an entirely different side of her. One he wanted to see a hell of a lot more of.

"Tell little sister I'm working on it, Mom. I'm working on it real hard."

* * * *

Tex knocked on Niki's door at 5:00 a.m. to pick her up the morning of Thanksgiving. She pulled the door opened and stepped aside. It took him a moment to catch his breath at the sight of her. She'd worn make-up and gathered her shoulder length hair into a loose knot on top of her head. A pair of jeans and a clingy, deep red, V-neck sweater never looked so good, especially matched with a pair of brown, knee-high leather boots. "Damn—I look like I crawled out of bed five minutes ago and you . . ." He stopped himself, afraid to sound like he was coming on to her. "You look beautiful, Nik."

She beamed at him. "Thanks, and you look fine, Tex. You want to help me load the pies? They're over there on the kitchen counter."

He swiveled and froze. "My mom asked you to bring six pies?"

She laughed. "No. She asked me to bring an apple, peach, or pecan pie. I brought two of each." She shrugged. "What can I say? Baking soothes me, and I had a rough week."

They were thirty minutes into the four hour drive to Beaumont when he risked asking about her week. "Are you having trouble adjusting to your new workplace?"

She opened her mouth to answer then closed it.

"I'm sorry. None of my business," he said.

She faced him. "It's not the work. I do the same work wherever I go. Same spreadsheets, different location is all. It's . . ." She faced the front again, stared out the windshield. "It's my supervisor I can't seem to—warm up to."

"What's the problem? Is he resentful of you transferring? Maybe he wanted to see someone else in that position?"

"I didn't say my supervisor hadn't warmed up to me."

It wasn't what she said as much as what she didn't that raised warning flags. "Has he made . . ." Tex paused, wanting to choose his words wisely. "Has he made improper advances towards you?"

"It's kind of a 'touchy-feely' situation."

Her softly murmured response had Tex seeing red. "Are you kidding me? It always amazes me that even in this day and age, there are still guys out there doing that."

She faced him head on. "Why are you assuming my supervisor is a guy?"

"Are you telling me a *female* supervisor is sexually harassing you?"

"It may not be as common but I'm sure it happens enough to be a statistic."

"I don't doubt that for a minute. It's all about power, and with more women than ever in positions of power it's bound to happen."

"I don't know. Maybe she's just super-friendly and I'm reading too much into it." Niki blew out her breath. "God, I miss my old supervisor—a happily married man whose wife I adored. But whatever—I can handle it."

"You shouldn't have to handle it." Tex slapped a hand on his steering wheel. "For crying out loud, doesn't your company have policies against sexual harassment? It should apply the same regarding all genders."

"I'm sure they do. But I'm the new girl and she's been there for twenty years."

"Would you put up with that behavior from a man?"

Niki bit her lower lip. "I'd have reported him already."

"Then why would you not report her? The situation may be a little different than what you're used to dealing with, but it's not acceptable behavior in the workplace—period."

She swiveled in her seat to face him, her eyes pleading. "Can we *please* talk about something else?"

He took a deep breath, held it a few moments before releasing it slowly. "What do you want to talk about?"

"How's that older couple who live in the house near the gate at the ranch?"

He cocked his head, trying to remember if he'd ever mentioned where Ms. Patsy and Mr. Ron lived. "How do you know where the Sedtals lived?"

Niki sucked in her breath. After a few moments, her head fell back against the seat. "I've been to that ranch once."

"That's impossible. I'm sure I'd know if you had."

"You weren't there. It was a couple of Easter Sunday's ago. I thought you lived in the house just inside the gate but I spoke to the older couple there and they told me you'd gone to Beaumont for the day. I—I asked them not to tell you I'd gone by because I was embarrassed."

Tex shifted his gaze back and forth between the road and Niki until the reality of the situation set in. He started to chuckle, which turned into a full-blown guffaw. "I'm sorry," he said, trying to catch his breath. "I'm not laughing at you, I swear, I'm not. It's only that I'd planned to drive down there to see you after the visit with my family. But then I spoke to Meagan and she said you'd left a note saying you were gone for the day. If I'd only known."

Her smile turned into contagious laughter and soon they were both laughing so hard they couldn't catch their breath.

"Damn, Nik—we really are a couple of dumbasses, aren't we?"

She wiped the tears from her eyes. "I think it's a communication problem—as in *lack of.* I had no idea at the time you lived in a cabin on that property."

"Yeah, as I said, I've made some improvements since then. All new windows and flooring, updated appliances, a big screened-in porch and I added a deck that looks out over the lake. The place has great views, but no wifi and only a half-ass decent cell phone service depending on the carrier."

"You live near a lake?"

"Yes, but only on one side of the cabin. It overlooks the Blanco River on the other side." He grinned. "You really need to come over and see for yourself. The view alone will blow you away. Do you like to fish?"

"I haven't been fishing since I was a kid and went with my dad. He always said I talked so much I scared the fish away."

"No way!" Tex chuckled. "It won't be a problem at my place. You said you're off the rest of the weekend, aren't you? Why don't you come over?" His heart beat double-time when she gave his suggestion a thoughtful nod.

"That sounds good."

Tex faced the front, trying not to grin like a high school kid after the homecoming queen said she'd go to prom with him. Maybe he'd finally have a chance at the one woman he'd never been able to get out of his mind.

* * * *

Niki eased out of the truck, a little stiff from the drive. A shout from behind had her turning in time to catch an excited Haley rushing at her.

"I'm so glad you're *here*!" Haley squealed as she hugged her tightly. She whispered in Niki's ear. "Please tell me the two of you are seeing each other again."

Niki hugged the girl she could easily see as a younger sister—or sister-in-law, even. "Just friends for now, but it's great to see you."

Haley pulled away to settle her brown eyed gaze on Niki. "For now? Maybe . . ." She tilted her head to one side, leaving Niki to ponder the suggestion.

Once she was certain Tex couldn't hear her, she answered the question. "We'll see." She looked up at the tall young man who joined them, his hair still neat and trimmed but this time sporting a thick beard. She pointed at his jaw. "Hey, Ben—is that your contribution to the 'No Shave November' theme for the month? It looks good on you." She accepted a hug from him.

"Except I've had it since the beginning of October. Happy Thanksgiving, Niki."

"Happy Thanksgiving to you also. How's married life treating you two?"

Ben looped his arm around Haley's waist and pulled her close. "I love it."

Haley settled her head against her husband's chest. "It's even better than I thought it would be." She grabbed Niki's hand and pulled her toward the opposite side of the truck. "Niki, this is our mom and dad."

Niki stared into the face of an older, but still pretty version of Haley. "Thank you so much for having me, Mr. and Mrs. Broussard."

"Oh, poo with that Mr. and Mrs. stuff, honey. Call us Angie and Ricky." Angie Broussard pulled her into a hug. "Welcome to our home, Niki! We are so thrilled you decided to come along."

She got the same treatment from the woman's husband, a tall, nice-looking man with salt and peppered hair, mustache, and beard. Tex and Haley had obviously inherited good looks from both their parents.

Ricky looked inside the back of the truck and rubbed his hands together. "Look at all the pies, hon—I'm hoping at least one of those is apple and has my name on it."

"Oh, thank goodness you brought dessert. My old oven has been giving me trouble lately." Angie's jaw dropped when Tex started handing off the six pies from the back of his truck. "I know you said you loved to bake, but are all of these homemade?"

Niki gave Angie an enthusiastic nod. "Yes, ma'am. I told Tex baking is therapy for me, and after the week I've had at work, I needed plenty of it."

Tex's dad reached for the two pies handed to him, his eyes glazing over. "Is it time for dessert yet?"

Niki smiled at the man. "No, but if you've got a pot of coffee ready, it sure would go well with a slice of that *apple* pie you've got in your right hand."

The man turned on his heel and headed to the house. "I'm putting a fresh pot on just for you, beautiful."

Niki watched his retreat and laughed. "I'm not sure if he was talking to me or the pie."

Angie gave her a gentle nudge. "Not that you aren't beautiful, but I really think he was talking to the pie."

Ricky turned at the door and shouted back at her. "It's nothing personal—it's pie!"

Niki gave him an enthusiastic 'OK' signal. "Yes sir, I understand completely. Carry on."

Tex stayed behind with her while the others walked ahead of them. "Hmph! You've been here less than five minutes and already have my family wrapped."

"Hey, I've got skills. I can make a lasting impression when I need to."

He paused at the door, one hand on the knob and stared down into her eyes. "You certainly made one on me. I'm glad you're here with me, Nik—seriously." He reached out with his free hand to stroke his fingers down one side of her face. "You've made my day."

Heat, scorching and tangible, radiated from the pit of her stomach to her chest, and moved up her neck into her cheeks. A frigid north breeze sent a whirlwind of leaves skittering at their feet as a mixture of conversations from inside the house carried out to them, mingling with the sounds of country life—a rooster crowing, hens cackling, the nicker of one or more horses, someone's dog barking in the distance. "Thank you for asking me. I'd be miserable and alone at my apartment if you hadn't."

"So, this is better?"

"Oh yeah—this is much better," she breathed, as he leaned in, inching his way closer until their lips nearly touched. He stopped suddenly, as though debating whether to continue or not. She took the guesswork out of his hands, completing the path for him, joining her lips to his in a soft and gentle kiss. She broke free from him once, hesitated, and went back for a second gentle kiss, ending with a soft nip to his lower lip. Deciding she'd controlled the court enough for one day, Niki pulled back, stopped short when Tex cupped the back of her head with his free hand. He deepened the kiss, melding his tongue with hers. She wrapped her right hand on the back of his neck, threading her fingers through the hair at his nape.

An odd-sounding *plop* punctuated Tex's low growl—followed by a groan as he pulled away to stare down at the pie he'd let slip onto the concrete walkway. Two dogs, one medium sized and spotted, and another large, solid black Labrador Retriever immediately moved in on the unexpected treat, gobbling up the splattered filling and crust. Tex muttered a string of low curses, ending with a distinct "Son of a bitch!"

Laughter rose in Niki's throat to burst from her mouth in uncontrolled sputtering. "Oh, my God. I can't believe you did that."

"I am so fu—flippin' sorry, Nik." He slapped one hand over his mouth and shook his head.

Angie stuck her head out the door. "What's all the commotion about?" She gasped when she saw the family pets munching down on the pie.

"I uh—I dropped the pie, Mom."

"Oh, your dad is not going to be happy about this. How'd you do that? You were a U.S. Marine for Christ's sake, Tex. You handled all kinds of state of the art equipment and machinery. You couldn't make it into the house with a single pie?"

Niki controlled her laughter and wiped her eyes. "It's my fault. I distracted him. But I baked two of each so we'll still have plenty."

The corners of Angie's mouth pulled down in a frown. "I sure hope that wasn't the second apple pie, because my husband is in the process of wolfing down a quarter of the other one."

"No, ma'am. It was one of the peach pies."

Tex's mom clucked her tongue as she shook her head. "What a waste. Honestly, I've never known you to be such a klutz, son." She faced Niki. "Whatever you did to distract him, you must have done well."

Tex cleared his throat, grumbling something that sounded like "Too damn well," before he turned on his heel and entered the house, leaving the two women alone outside the door.

Angie placed her hand on Niki's arm. "Nicole, I want you to know that I haven't seen my son this affected by a woman since he took Penelope Adams to prom his senior year." She looped her arm through Niki's and led her into a house bursting with country warmth and charm. "Whatever you're doing, keep it up—it's nice to see him happy. But I hope he makes you just as happy."

"Yes ma'am." Niki spotted Tex standing beside Ben and Haley, all three gathered in front of a large TV set mounted on the living room wall to watch the Thanksgiving Day parade. She faced his mom again. "What happened with Penelope?"

"She broke his heart—ditched him at the prom to go parking with his best friend."

"Oh!" she gasped. "That is so wrong!"

"Poor Tex was crazy about that girl. Swore he'd never let a woman get to him like that again." She gazed at her son, her cheek creased in a familiar grin. Tex's dimples may have come from his dad, but his smile definitely showed traces of his mom. Angie faced Niki again. "My boy may have won a few battles over the years, but I believe he's just lost the war."

Niki clamped her lips together, refusing to hope just yet that what she and Tex shared was more than friendship.

Angie pulled her close and whispered in her ear. "It's okay if you don't believe it yet, honey. I have enough faith for both of us."

Chapter 4

They'd left his parents place by 6:00 p.m., with Niki promising to visit again. She stared out into the darkness of the late November sky, contemplating the day spent with Tex's family. From the second she'd entered their house Niki had felt completely at home. A peacefulness she hadn't felt since before her dad's stroke drifted over her like soft clouds. It transitioned into drowsiness and she closed her eyes for a moment . . .

By the time she woke, startled, she knew from the trail of drool down her chin she'd been out awhile. Slightly disoriented, she wiped her chin and cleared her throat as she sat up. Thank God the inside of the truck was too dark for Tex to see.

"Did you sleep well?"

She looked over at his profile, praying she hadn't snored or anything in her sleep. "I did. I didn't realize how tired I was." She looked at the clock on his dash and sucked in her breath when she saw it was nearly 9:00 p.m. "I'm so sorry, Tex. I can't believe I slept so long. We're nearly home—my home, anyway."

"Don't apologize. It gave me time to do some thinking."

Thinking? About what? That could mean anything. Her mind turned into a whirlwind of speculations. Had he come up with reasons he shouldn't have asked her along? She sat there for a couple of minutes more in silence, her mind flitting from one scenario to another as her imagination worked overtime.

"Earth to Niki."

His rumbled comment got her attention. She faced him. "What?"

"You look like you've got something on your mind. Are you alright over there?"

She nodded. "I'm good." She tried to think of something to say that wouldn't make her sound like a semi-conscious lunatic. The conversation with his mom over his disastrous prom date fueled her curiosity. "You ever hear from Penelope Adams?"

He swiveled his head to look at her, the dashboard lights illuminating his handsome face. "Who the hell told you about—uh—Mom . . ." He shook his head slowly. "Please don't tell me she gave you the 'don't hurt my baby boy' speech."

Niki smiled. "Not at all. I think it was her way of explaining your past behavior."

"You mean the fact that I was a top notch asshole? I don't blame that on anyone but myself."

Excellent answer Cowboy—shows a level of growth and maturity you definitely lacked before.

"So, you're not still milking the old 'I'll never give my heart to a woman again' excuse?"

"Hell, Nik . . . it's too late for that."

She studied his profile. Had he found someone else back in Blanco? "What do you mean?"

He removed one hand from the steering wheel and used it to smooth down his goatee. He always did that when he was nervous. "There's something I haven't told you."

Damn. Here it comes. He's going to bare his soul to her about the new woman in his life. She prepared herself to act happy for him.

"I made a trip down to Louisiana several months ago, especially to see you."

She turned, stared at his profile again. "You did?" Her heart hammered in her chest as his head bobbed in acknowledgment.

"Your roommate told me you'd moved to St. Louis for good."

She swallowed the lump in her throat. She'd had to move quickly after her dad got sick. "Did you have a specific reason?"

"I did." He put his signal light on to turn onto the street for her subdivision. "Now that I've opened this can o' worms, I'm thinking maybe I should have waited a few minutes more." They drove a ways in silence until he turned his truck into her driveway. He threw it in park and turned off the engine.

Tex took a deep breath and blew it out slowly as he faced her. "The fact is, I've never been able to forget you, Nik. Those two nights we spent together, the days in between—and all the times afterward, seeing you with Bo McAllister. I've never stopped thinking about what I could have had with you."

They both reached for their seatbelts at the same time, met over his truck's console in a searing kiss—the kind that righted wrongs, healed hurts, and put all mistakes in the past. He pulled back, his hands on her face, and touched his forehead to hers. "I want you in my life, Nicole. Is it too late?"

She blinked back tears and shook her head. "Not if you meant everything you just said to me."

He placed a gentle kiss on her forehead, one on each of her closed eyelids and her nose before sealing it with a kiss to her lips. "God, I do. I mean every word of it."

She smiled through her tears. "Then come inside with me?" She wrapped her hands around the back of his neck and tunneled her fingers through his hair. He closed his eyes, letting her fingers work their magic as she massaged the back of his head. His low growl rumbled through the truck before it transitioned into a groan.

He brought his head forward to settle his gaze on her. "I'd love to, Nik, but I have things to tend to at my place. Would you mind terribly grabbing whatever you need and coming to my cabin with me?"

Tex cocked his head slightly, drawing her gaze to one delectable dimple, only to have the strong jawline grab her attention seconds later. "Okay," she breathed. "Give me five minutes." He got out of the truck first, opened the passenger side and helped her down. "Do you want to wait inside?" Need tugged at her—she wondered how much longer she could keep her hands to herself.

He looped his arm around her lower back and pulled her close for another mind-blowing kiss. "No," he said, stepping back and out of her reach. "I'd better stay out here and cool off or we may never leave. Hurry back, okay?"

"Uh huh," Niki hurried to her house, unlocked the door with shaky fingers and closed it behind her. She pulled an overnight case from her closet and threw a few pieces of clothes inside. Inside her bathroom, she grabbed her makeup case from her vanity and dumped several items into it, remembering her toothbrush at the last second. She zipped it up and stared at her flushed reflection in the bathroom mirror. "Get a grip, girl. It's not like you've never been with the man before."

Oh but she definitely had. She thought back to how good it had been with Tex and gripped the edges of the sink before her knees turned to jelly at the memories. All doubts behind her, she tucked the case under her arm and grabbed her overnight bag on the way out of her apartment. She locked the door and headed toward the tall Texan leaning casually against his bright red pickup. He straightened at her approach and opened the door before grabbing her bags from her. He helped her inside and carried the bags around to his side of the truck.

When they'd both settled into their seats he faced her. "Are you sure about this? I don't want you to have any regrets later."

She swallowed the lump in her throat. "Are you planning to do something to make me have regrets, Cowboy?"

He leaned toward her purposefully. "My only goal is to make you regret leaving me."

Oh. Dear. God! Stupefied into silence, she faced the front and remained quiet during the trip to his place. They reached the home near the arched entrance to the ranch and she noticed how bare and empty it looked. "You said the old couple is in a retirement home?"

"Yeah, for now. I'm not sure if that's temporary or not. It's in San Marcos, though. Not far at all. I think three of their five living children are around there."

She nodded, tucking that piece of information away for future reference. The drive progressed to a slightly bumpier ride once they passed the first house and left the main road. A few minutes later they pulled up to a rustic looking cabin on tall pilings. It stood out against the backdrop of the November sky, the light from an attached screened-in porch glowing like a navigational beacon in the darkness of the night. She opened her passenger door, paused at Tex's next words.

"Wait until I get over there to help you. It's tricky if you don't know where you're going."

No argument from her. Cloud coverage obliterated what little light the waxing crescent moon would have emitted. He came around to her side and pulled the door open, taking her hand to help her out of the truck.

"Jesus, it's dark as sin out here." Her words carried in the wide open space.

"Tonight it is. Give it another week and clear skies and you'll be able to read a book out here at this time. If it wasn't so cloudy tonight you'd be able to see some stars. Loop your arm around mine and follow me." He shouldered her bags and balanced a few containers of leftovers his mom had sent home with him. Together they made their way up a path to a set of stairs leading to his front door. "Excuse the mess," he said, unlocking his door and pushing it open for her to walk inside. "I didn't have much time to clean up after myself this morning and I sure as hell wasn't expecting company."

"No problem." She stood in one spot until he emptied his armload of items and flipped on a light. Niki gasped at the interior of the spacious cabin, surprised at the comfy feel of the place as well as the size. "This is nice, Tex. When you described it as rustic I was expecting something more . . ."

"Primitive?" he finished for her.

She laughed. "I guess so, but this is a great space you've created for yourself."

He beamed, clearly pleased with her initial reaction. "I've got to go tend to my horse. Will you be alright here for a few minutes? If I don't go make my round I'll pay hell for it tomorrow."

She smiled and nodded, remembering his tale about his temperamental horse, Captain Perry. "Sure. Go on and do whatever you have to."

Niki used her time alone to explore his man cave, truly impressed with what he'd done with the place. He'd told her it was his work in progress and she could see signs of his handiwork everywhere, from new stainless appliances in the modern kitchen full of pine cabinetry that boasted tons of storage from open shelving. The countertops were also wood, with images of horseshoes, longhorns, and what she assumed was a brand burned into the wood, and sealed with a thick clear epoxy coating that glistened like glass. A round table with four chairs filled the space between the kitchen and open living area covered in weathered wood planking.

High quality leather furniture, masculine in style but eye-pleasing none-the-less, fit perfectly in the room, accented with heavy wooden end tables. Huge windows filled the majority of wall space, no doubt allowing glorious amounts of light into the room during the daylight hours. Now the great gaping spaces of black only reflected items in the room's lit interior.

She picked up her two bags and explored the rest of the cabin. A flip of a wall switch had her staring at a massive bed in the only bedroom in the place. She passed her hand over the bulky wood of what looked to be a handmade headboard, wondering about the craftsman's identity. She found the bathroom, approving of its modern and obviously new walk-in shower, lined with natural-looking stone and tile. She took the time to freshen up, finishing just as Tex let himself back into the cabin.

He stood at the door and used a boot jack to remove his mud-crusted boots, looked up and smiled at her when she re-entered the living room. "You find everything you need?"

"Mostly." She leaned against one end of the kitchen cabinet. "I'm waiting on you to take care of the rest of my needs."

He approached but stopped in front of her to lift his hands. "Give me a few minutes to wash the horse off of me and I'll see what I can do to take care of that."

She bit her bottom lip and nodded. "Hurry."

"Yes ma'am." He made a bee-line for his bathroom and shut the door.

Niki paced impatiently, muttering at the sound of prolonged running water. "What the hell is taking him so long?" Seconds after she returned to the living room the bathroom door opened. She did an abrupt about face and entered the bedroom and froze at the sight of a naked-from-the-waist-up Tex pulling a shirt from his closet. Her breath caught at the sight of his beautiful broad chest and shoulders, all ripped with definition—begging for her touch. She swallowed hard, and managed to speak. "Don't bother with that shirt."

Tex faced her. "Well, shit . . ." The blue and white plaid shirt in his hands fell to the floor in a heap of flannel.

She approached slowly. "What's wrong?"

"N-nothing's wrong. It's just that I've been fantasizing about this very thing for a couple of years, and now that it's here I kind of feel like an inexperienced teenager."

She stopped in front of him and smiled. "I wouldn't worry about it if I were you. I have a feeling it'll all fall into place soon." Her palms flattened against his chest, she purred at the feel of his bare skin beneath her hands. He brought his hands up to her waist and pulled her against him. She sucked in her breath as his pectorals tightened under her palms, the light covering of blonde hair on his chest tickling her fingertips. This man owned his body like no one else, his muscles tight and corded, rippling with power. He'd looked like Adonis years before but now . . . "Ranching seems to agree with you."

He grinned. "In all fairness, I'd kind of let myself go back when you first met me. I went through this phase of too much alcohol and not enough working out. I joined a gym in Blanco and between that and helping out on this ranch I manage to stay in shape. It's hard work, but it gives me a sense of peace I needed in my life." Tex's smile faded as his head fell forward.

Niki suspected he was reliving some of the horrors he'd experienced in the Middle East and her heart broke for him. Now that she thought about it, their reasons for relocating were different but the same. She'd run *from* Missouri to escape painful memories of her parents. He'd run *to* Blanco, to his dead friend's home to escape the pain of losing him. She placed her hands on both sides of his face, raised his chin until she could see straight into his beautiful eyes. "Tex, we've never discussed any of the things you experienced when you were an active duty Marine . . ."

He squeezed his eyes shut and cocked his head to one side. "And I don't want to now."

She sensed him resisting, raising a barrier against his emotions—an invisible one, but there none the less. She caressed his face with both hands and drew him forward again. "But do you need to?"

* * * *

Tex tried to remain closed-off, even attempted to be the slightest bit angry with her for bring up things better left alone. One look into the soul-searching depth of those gorgeous green eyes had him questioning himself. Something about the feel of her hands on his face, cradling him, had him wanting to open up to her. Maybe he'd carried the horrors around with him long enough. He couldn't speak—could only give her the barest of nods before she picked up his shirt from the floor and handed it to him.

"Put this on," she said, shaking her head at the shape he was in. "Jesus, Tex. You could be a body double for Chris Hemsworth in the latest *Thor* movie. Those six-pack abs are far too distracting for a serious conversation."

Tex slipped his arms into the sleeves, somewhat surprised when she pushed his hands away so she could button him up herself. She took his hand and led him to the leather couch in the living room. He settled himself on one end and she snuggled up close to him, her back to his chest. He wrapped both arms around her, sighed when she rested her head against his chest. He sat in silence for a full minute, gathering his thoughts, comforted by the feel of her in his arms.

"We lost some good men over there, Nik. But when you sign up you expect that. What I didn't expect to see was what some of those civilians suffered at the hands of their own people— sometimes their own family members."

Several moments passed before Niki responded with a soft, "I'm here to listen if you want to share with me."

Tex started slowly, hesitantly—telling her about the horrors he'd seen caused by children coming up on various forms of IEDs. He spoke of carrying children to their medics with limbs blown off. Of seeing children wired with explosives by the Taliban. As horrible as that had been, nothing had ever touched him like the Somalian incident.

He hesitated, wondering if he could speak about something he hadn't dared to attempt to put into words before now. Tex swallowed the huge lump in his throat, the one that always appeared when he thought about that fragile girl he'd discovered behind a pile of rubble, beaten bloody, her face disfigured. He told Niki how the girl revealed the story to their translator. How she'd been disfigured by her own father because he blamed *her* for being raped by a gang of men from a nearby village. By the end of that story his voice was thick with emotion.

He sighed, wiping away tears he couldn't seem to stop from running down his face. "You can't imagine the horrors the women and children are subjected to over there by the same people who should be protecting them. It's . . ." He stopped, gave his throat a rough clearing before trying to finish. "It's a harsh, hostile environment for women and children." He shook his head. "I hated every minute of being there."

They sat a few moments in silence before she turned to face him, her own face streaked with tears. He reached out to brush them away. "I'm sorry for making you cry, Nik."

She kissed the inside of his palms and gave him a sad little smile. "Please don't be sorry. I'm glad you shared your experience with me. My only hope is that it helped you to talk about it."

Tex closed his eyes and took several deep breaths, released them slowly. With the final exhale, he experienced a release, a definite lifting of his spirit as he let the horrors of the past go. By the time he opened his eyes, his conscience clear, his soul lighter than it had been in over twenty years. His eyes widened.

"Better?"

He nodded before hugging her tightly to him. "Much better," he whispered into her hair. He released her then and took her face in his two hands. "Thank you, Nicole."

"You're welcome."

She leaned forward and placed a gentle kiss on his lips before rising from the couch. She stood before him, her hand extended. He stood and took it, letting her lead him to his own bedroom. He undressed her with a patience he didn't know he'd possessed until that moment, reveling in the sight, finding joy in the act of baring all that beautiful skin of hers. She removed his clothes and pushed him gently onto the bed.

She took control then, mounting him, touching … tasting … kissing … until he thought he'd burst from wanting her. Only then did she lift herself and settle, burying him deep inside her. She moved slowly, allowing their passions to build to a slow crescendo—finally, blessedly, ending with her crying out in pleasure as she reached her plateau. Only then did he join her, unable to hold back as he shouted her name in a soul-satisfying, crashing, burst of completion.

He lay there afterwards, his arms around her limp torso, trying to comprehend the level of intensity their lovemaking had taken on. "Nicole . . ." he gasped.

"I know, Tex—I know." She untangled herself from him and slid to one side, resting her face on his chest.

Everything inside him told him he'd just experienced something new, something alien to him. Tex possessed an impressive list of experiences with women—he'd had an awful lot of *sex* in his lifetime. Until this moment, he'd never really made love to a woman. He'd never had the kind of spiritual connection during a sexual experience as he'd just had with Nicole. Even back when they'd first met, as good as it had been it had only been sex. This had transported him to an entirely different level of play. Just for a moment his male bravado instincts told him to run like hell. Thankfully, and before he could screw it up too badly, his brain reminded him of his lonely existence before Niki's return.

He wrapped one arm around her, pulling her closer, curled his leg around hers in a purely possessive move.

"What just happened?" she said, her panting finally receding to some semblance of normal breathing.

"I'm not sure." What a liar—he damn well knew what happened. Some part of him resisted saying the words—resisted admitting out loud that he was undeniably in love with Nicole Reeves.

They lay in his bed, listening to the sounds of the night, the far off yipping of a coyote, cattle calling out to one another, an owl in a nearby tree. He lay there, silent and still, until Niki's breathing let him know she'd fallen asleep. He closed his eyes, sensing a shift in their relationship, and wondered if he was up to the challenge.

Chapter 5

Niki woke to soft lips pressed against hers. She raised her arms around Tex's neck, curled her fingers in hair still damp from a recent shower, releasing the scent of something fresh and masculine. "Um, you smell good." She covered her mouth. "And I probably have dragon breath."

He waved a mug of coffee under her nose. "That's what this is for." He slapped her lightly on the butt. "Come on, Nik. I've got something I want to show you. You want to get up now?"

She stretched, groaning at the memory of their recent lovemaking. "I guess. What time is it, anyway?"

"It's still early, but I want you to come with me just for a minute. After that, if you still want to, you can crawl back into bed."

She sat up and took the mug of coffee from him, curious about his cryptic suggestion. She took a sip. "Mm, that's good. Strong, just the way I like it." She swung her legs out of the bed and sat up, clutching the sheet to her bare breast as goose bumps formed on her skin in the chill of the cabin. "Give me a minute to put some clothes on."

"Hurry, I don't want you to miss it." He walked out of the room, a mysterious grin on his face.

Niki grabbed her clothes and went into the bathroom, breathing in the aroma of Tex, courtesy of his men's body wash. She was out in five minutes, wearing her clothes from the day before. Her coffee mug in hand, she exited the bedroom, stopped just inside the living room to admire the glorious sight that greeted her. Windows that had shown nothing but pitch black last night were now a showcase for the beauty of Texas hill country.

"Oh, my sweet lord—this view is perfection."

Tex smiled, obviously pleased at her reaction. He took her hand and led her to the cabin's back door and out to a huge wrap around deck. "Don't say anything," he whispered, as he pointed to a spot at ground level.

Niki looked down at a cluster of deer nibbling on shrubs near the bank of the river. "Oh ..." she breathed, careful to keep her voice down. Tex pointed in another direction and her gaze followed, finding a pair of raccoons. She sipped her coffee and watched, fascinated by the raccoon's antics. She walked from one end of the deck to the other, taking the time to study some of Mother Nature's finest displays. "Good Lord, Tex. No wonder you love it here. It's . . ." She lifted one hand and let if fall, unable to come up with a phrase worthy enough for the sight before her.

After a moment he spoke, his tone filled with a touch of reverence. "This is my church."

She nodded. "I can see that." She turned, leaned against the railing to study his face. "Is it your place of confession, too?"

He stepped forward, took her coffee cup from her and placed it on the railing before closing the gap between them. Slipping his hands around her waist he pulled her close. "Sometimes. But I haven't had a whole hell of a lot to confess since I've been here."

She tilted her head, contemplating his answer. "I don't know whether to feel good or bad about that."

He chuckled before planting a kiss on her that stirred the smoldering embers of desire. She groaned when he pulled away. "Keep that up and you won't get much work done around here today."

He smiled and planted a second. "That's the point," he growled at the end of it.

She took his hand and led him inside the cabin back toward his bedroom and the sheet-rumpled king-size bed, pausing before it. "No fair. You had time to take a shower."

His right cheek creased with a one-sided grin. "We can remedy that easy enough." He pulled her into the bathroom, turned on the shower taps before undressing her. "Take your time," he said, before leaving her to it.

Niki grabbed three travel size bottles of shower gel, shampoo, and conditioner from her bag before stepping under the hot stream of water. She washed and conditioned her hair quickly, had just lathered the washcloth he'd provided with gel when the door opened and he joined her. Her pulse quickened at the sight of his gloriously naked body. "My first thought when I saw this shower was that it was big enough for two."

"That's why I designed it this way, but it's the first time since I've built it that I have a chance to test it out."

"You haven't brought anyone up here before me?"

"That's a negative."

"And you built this yourself?"

He nodded and wiggled his fingers. "These hands are good for more than just giving pleasure, you know."

Her laughter rang out loudly against the tiled walls. "Someone's feeling mighty proud of himself."

He stepped closer, hard and on full display. "Is this proud enough for you?"

This time she eliminated the space between them, slid her soapy hands over his hard, smooth butt cheeks.

But Tex had apparently come to play hard ball. He propped one foot on the built-in shower seat and draped her right leg over his knee. Shifting his left arm around her back to support her, he moved his free hand between her legs.

"Tex . . ." she breathed. "That feels—so good."

He grinned, kissed her before moving to her neck and answering in a low growl. "Good ain't exactly my goal, Nicole."

She smiled. "I love the way you say my name."

"Mm … Ni-coo-lle," he drawled, drawing it out as he found the spot. The sweet spot that only men who cared about giving pleasure to a woman dared to find. "Tell me when you're close," he said, his breath hot against her ear.

"Uh huh …" She closed her eyes as sweet waves of heat and pleasure increased, widening, building, bringing her closer to where she wanted to be—to where she *needed* to be. She focused on the sound of water hitting Tex's broad back, splashing over the tiles as the rhythm of his fingers increased. "Yeesss . . ." she hissed, incapable of any other speech. Close—closer—too damn close. "Tex!"

One slight shift of his position and he was deep inside her. She gasped at the sensation, the shock of having him buried to the hilt in an instant. He moved in long, smooth strokes that had her reaching her climax in seconds and crying out with her release. Niki sunk her nails into his back as he pounded harder in the effort to reach his. He finished with a low growl from deep in his chest as he pumped into her.

Tex held her closer until his breathing returned to normal. He pressed a kiss against her forehead then another, just as gentle, to her lips. He pulled back far enough to level a sincere, blue-eyed gaze on her. "God, I missed you, Nicole. Stay here with me the rest of the weekend."

"Tex, I shouldn't—"

He silenced her with a heart-wrenching look. "Please, Nik."

She cupped his handsome face between her hands. The man was down-right dangerous under normal circumstances. "You aren't playing fair."

"I don't worry about playing fair—not when I'm playing for keeps."

She sucked in her breath as he brushed his right thumb pad lightly over her left nipple, sending a message that there was plenty more where that came from. Well, damn. How the hell could she say no to that?

* * * *

They'd just cleaned the kitchen after breakfast when Tex leaned against the counter, his arms crossed against his chest as he contemplated something that had been running through his mind. "Would you mind coming with me to pay the Sedtals a visit in San Marcos? I think I told you they've been staying in an assisted living complex for a while."

"After his stroke," she finished for him. "Has he recovered?"

"Oh, yeah. He's doing great. I got close to them while they were here. I used to check up on them pretty often and Ms. Patsy always insisted I come in for coffee and whatever baked goods she had on hand. I'd planned to go by and wish them a Happy Thanksgiving. I usually stop off at a bakery and pick up some cookies or something."

She beamed at his suggestion. "When did you plan to leave? I'd love to bake something homemade for them. They seemed like a sweet couple."

"I'm not sure what you can scrounge up in here to use for ingredients, but I thought we could leave around 10:00 a.m., get in a quick visit and I could take you to lunch over there afterwards."

Niki did a quick check of his pantry and pulled out several ingredients for no-bake oatmeal cookies and peanut butter cookies. She eyed him skeptically. "They aren't diabetics or allergic to nuts, are they?"

"Not to my knowledge." She gave him a brief nod and he watched, completely amazed at how quickly she whipped up the two separate recipes. They were packaged and ready for delivery in less than an hour. One hour later they were knocking on the door of the Sedtal's third floor apartment.

Ms. Patsy answered, her face breaking into a wide smile when she saw him. "Hey, Matthew! I just told Ron I expected to see you sometime today."

"I've brought someone along for you to meet. This is Nicole Reeves."

Niki extended her hand. "Hello Mrs. Sedtal. We did meet briefly a couple of years ago, but I'm sure you don't remember the incident."

Patsy's eyes narrowed as though searching her memory banks for something. Her eyes lit up suddenly. "Oh, but I do remember. You showed up on Easter Sunday and asked me not to tell this young man you'd been there."

Niki nodded. "Yes ma'am, that's right."

Patsy's gaze went from Niki, to Tex, and back to Niki. "I'm glad the two of you finally got your wires uncrossed. You make a beautiful couple."

Tex resisted the urge to pull Niki close out of respect for both women. For some damn reason he found it difficult to keep his hands to himself when Nicole was anywhere within his reach. Her welcoming response to his advances made the situation even worse. Mr. Ron entered the room with a loud clearing of his throat, rescuing them all from a potentially embarrassing situation.

"Tex! My beautiful wife said we could expect to see you soon. I don't know why I bother questioning her."

Patsy patted her husband's arm. "I don't either, Ron." She winked at Niki. "You'd think by now, he'd have learned to say 'Yes dear' and keep his mouth shut, right?"

Niki laughed before extending her hand to the man and introducing herself.

Ronald Sedtal took her hand, his eyes creased with laughter. "One of these days I'll learn. Y'all come on in." He pointed to the containers in Tex's arms. "My goody senses are detecting something tasty. What'd you bring me, Tex?"

Tex didn't bother answering, but opened the two containers to show him.

Ms. Patsy threw her arms in the air. "Peanut butter cookies are his favorite, and I love these no bake oatmeal cookies. I'm putting a pot of coffee on right now!"

Tex followed Mr. Ron out onto their small balcony area where he had several planters filled with winter vegetable plants. Once the exterior door had closed behind them the older man turned toward him. "It's about time you settle down, Tex. You had Patsy worried for a while that you'd never find anyone to put up with you. You don't want to end up a lonely old bachelor, do you?"

Tex laughed at the man's bluntness. "I used to think I did." He stared through the glass panes of the door into the living room of the Sedtal's third story apartment. The two women were already sitting side by side and talking as though they'd known each other for years. "Now I know differently."

Mr. Ron's grin turned into a rumbling belly laugh. "Yeah, the right woman will do that to you." He nudged Tex with his elbow and nodded toward the women. "Don't you let that one get away. She's a looker for sure, but more importantly, she's a good person and it's obvious she cares about you." He gave him a wink. "I bet the two of you create quite a bit of sparks together."

Tex laughed at his insinuation. "Come on now, Mr. Ron. You know a gentleman never kisses and tells."

The man nodded. "You mean she's turned you into a gentleman? Now that *is* a good sign!"

Tex sent one last glance at Niki before turning away. "Yes sir, I guess it is."

Chapter 6

December 22nd

Niki pulled out her ringing cell phone before throwing her purse on the seat of her car. Her heart fluttered in her chest at the sight of Tex's handsome face flashing across her phone's screen. "How did you know I needed to hear the sound of your voice right now?"

"I didn't, but I sure as hell needed to hear yours. What's up, babe? You sound stressed."

"I had to cut my lunch short. I've been *summoned* for a one-on-one with my supervisor."

"Which one—the older man on his third wife or the gay lady with the hots for you?"

"Stop it … I don't know that for sure."

He was quiet for a few seconds. "Nik, if there was one thing I learned in the Marines, it's never to underestimate the enemy. Everything you've told me about this woman screams manipulation. Is there any way you can get out of being alone with her in that room?"

Niki started her car and backed out of the restaurant's parking lot. "I'm afraid not. I'll be alright, Tex. I can handle myself. If worse comes to worse, I'll walk away from the job."

"Please do something to protect yourself. Get one of those tiny cameras and place it somewhere inconspicuous. It'd be a damn shame for you to lose a job because your supervisor lacks a sense of personal boundaries."

She took a deep breath, her stomach growing queasier with each block closer to her office. She'd told herself the same thing a number of times already. "Please change the subject."

"I called because Mom wants to know what kind of pies we're bringing over."

"I planned to bake the same thing I brought for Thanksgiving. Should I bake an extra one for the family dogs?"

"Oh, you're funny. Are they baked yet?"

"I haven't even started them. I thought I could bring all the ingredients to your place and bake them there. Your kitchen is so much nicer than mine."

"Oh good, I don't have to beg. I really wanted to see you tonight."

"If I'd have known you were ready to beg I'd have held out."

"Held out for what?"

She chuckled. "I don't know … a little more."

"I've got a lot more of what you need waiting for you right here. You need me to pick you up at your place?"

"No, I'll load up my car and meet you at the Sedtal's place just inside the gate."

"Sounds good. Can't wait to see you."

She pulled into the parking garage and threw her car into park, wishing she'd driven someplace a little further away for lunch. "I'm back at work already, sweetie. I need to let you go."

"Nik, seriously. I've got a bad feeling about this meeting of yours. Please be careful."

She locked her car and headed across to the multi-leveled office complex. "I will. I promise."

"I'll be here at the cabin for the next hour if you need to talk; and if you need me over there, let me know. I'll drop what I'm doing and drive like a bat out of hell to get to you."

"My hero." She stopped in front of the steps of the building, amazed at the change in Tex since she'd first met him. They'd spent every weekend together since Thanksgiving and each Sunday when she had to leave him was more difficult than the previous. "Have I told you lately how much I appreciate your support?"

"Yeah," he drawled. "But I never get tired of hearing it. Feels good knowing I'm helping you out."

She grinned as she approached the elevator and hit the up button. "I'll be getting on the elevator soon and I'll have to end the call."

"I understand. Did you ever put up any of your mom's Christmas decorations?"

Her heart ached with the familiar pain. The plastic storage containers full of Christmas decorations were exactly where Tex had stored them for her, still stacked in a pile in her shed. She hadn't summoned enough heart or courage to look at them, much less drag them out and empty the contents of each one. The thought of seeing her mom's decorations spread throughout any place but her parents' home wasn't something she was ready to face. "No. Did you put up a tree in your cabin?" Tex claimed he wasn't much on putting up anything that he'd have to turn around and take down.

"And risk invalidating my man card? Absolutely not," he grumbled.

The ding of a bell signaled the elevator car's arrival. "I'll talk to you later."

"Later, babe."

She turned off her phone and stepped into the elevator, the sound of his voice still echoing in her mind. In the past she'd hated it when guys had called her 'Babe'. But the sound of the word rolling off Matthew Houston Broussard's tongue made her want to curl up in a ball beside him and purr with pure satisfaction. She stepped off onto the third floor corridor and approached the office of B.L. McKenna.

She stood for a moment, searching her phone for something, when the door to the women's executive restroom opened and closed behind her. The feel of someone's hand to her lower back, just above her butt had her stiffening and pulling away from the intrusive touch. She hugged her phone close to her chest and pivoted to face her supervisor, B.L.

"What do you have there?"

"Checking my phone messages," Niki said, amazed at the woman's lack of professionalism.

The woman sauntered into her office, her long legs tanned and every bit as toned and shapely as the rest of her body. Her long dark hair fell straight down her back like black silk. She turned at the door to look back at Niki with exotically shaped eyes so dark brown they looked nearly black. "Are you coming?"

Niki lifted her phone. "I've got five minutes. I'll be there as soon as I'm finished with this text." The woman was a genius at what she did. So why the hell couldn't B.L. comprehend Niki's complete lack of interest in members of the same sex? Not now. Not ever.

"Don't keep me waiting," B.L. said, turning and heading to her desk, swinging her hips, her short, tight skirt hugging her butt in open invitation.

Niki frowned, aware that B.L. had worn modest black slacks at the business meeting this morning. She fiddled with her phone and dropped it into the shallow pocket of her short jacket before entering the woman's office.

B.L. looked up from her black leather desk chair and smiled. "Close the door please."

"Are you planning to fire me or reprimand me for not performing my duties as expected when I was hired?"

Her supervisor blinked. "Not at all."

"Then I'd prefer to keep it open," Niki said.

B.L. smiled sweetly, rose from her chair and walked around her clutter-free desk to the door. She closed it and turned to face Niki, the smile replaced with a predatory leer. "My office, honey—my rules."

Every instinct in Niki told her to run like hell—get out of that office as fast as she could. But she stayed. For every employee who'd ever felt betrayed and taken advantage of by anyone in a position of power, be they man or woman, she stayed to face-off with the dragon. She stood tall and crossed her arms tightly against her chest, ready to come out swinging if she must. "I've got work waiting for me on my desk, Ms. McKenna. What is it you need from me?"

The woman approached. "I've asked you to call me B.L."

"I'm more comfortable calling you Ms. McKenna. I don't believe there's any kind of company policy against that, is there?"

"Of course not, I just like members of my team to be more at ease in the work environment."

On a scale of one to ten, Niki's level of ease had dipped far into the negative values. She'd be more likely to call this woman by her given name of Betty Lou before she'd call her B.L. "Did you cut my lunch short for a specific reason?"

"Yes. I wanted to ask if you skied."

"Water or snow?"

"Snow of course."

"I've been a couple of times. I'm not very good at it." *B.L. wasn't really going to cross that line, was she?*

"I've got a cabin reserved in Steamboat over the holidays. I'm looking for a travelling companion. All expenses paid."

She crossed it. "Thank you but I'm not interested."

"Are you sure? It could become quite a lucrative move for you."

"Are you insinuating you'd do more for me here in the company if I were to go with you?"

"I'm saying it wouldn't hurt."

"And if I don't, would you hold me back?"

B.L. only shrugged.

"I have plans over the holidays. I'm going with my *boyfriend* to visit his family."

"You'd have much more fun with me."

Niki smiled. "I know for a fact I wouldn't. Really, thank you for the offer, but my answer is no." She lowered her arms to her sides. "Is that all you needed?"

B.L. closed the gap between them in a flash, pushing Niki backward against the glass topped surface of her desk so hard she lost her balance and had to scramble to keep from falling. B.L. made quick work of Niki's disadvantage. She slid one hand up Niki's skirt and groped her breast with the opposite.

Niki's shock fell way to cold, stark anger as she shoved at the woman with all her might. "Get off of me—now!" She struggled to get her footing back, finally stood tall—still panting with the exertion as well as pure indignation. "What the hell is wrong with you? Isn't it bad enough that women have had to put up with this crap from men? Don't you have the slightest sense of female solidarity?"

"What I have is a strong sense that you want me. That man of yours can't do for you what I can—in bed or out of it. I can make sure you go straight to the top in this company." She lunged for her again.

This time Niki was ready for her. She came across with a right hook, clipping B.L. on the left cheek with a shot that would most likely leave the bitch with a black eye.

Betty Lou McKenna stood there, one hand on her cheek, staring in shock at Niki. "You screwed up, big time, honey. You'd just as soon pack up your desk now."

Niki got nose to nose with the woman. "Let me tell you something, *Betty Lou*. I wouldn't take that kind of repulsive behavior from a man, and I sure as shit won't take it from you. And the only person who can call me honey is a six and a half foot tall retired Marine who gave me some pretty good advice about not underestimating my enemy." She turned and stormed off to the door, irate and shaking with rage.

"Don't bother going back to your office. You're fired!" B.L. sneered after her. "I'm calling security right now to have you escorted out of the building. And I *will* be pressing charges for assault. No witnesses. It'll be your word against mine and I've got seniority."

Niki walked to the elevator and hit the button. The doors opened immediately with a quiet *swish*. "You do what you've gotta do, Betty Lou." She pulled her phone from her pocket. "And I'll do the same." She tapped a button to stop the recording and stepped into the elevator. She didn't bother going down to her own desk, sure the woman would make good on her call to security. Instead she went straight to the top floor, praying someone would be around to hear her out. She played back part of the message, satisfied with the quality of the recording and smiled all the way to the top floor.

* * * *

She buckled herself into her car, mentally drained from the afternoon of finger pointing, playing the blame game and finally, negotiations. She started her car and called Tex to give him the abbreviated version of her afternoon.

As suspected, B.L.'s supervisor was none too pleased to hear her complaints against his prized employee of twenty years. He didn't want to believe it, but had no choice when faced with the blatant evidence, even then insisting this had been the first complaint against B.L.

Within ten minutes of sending a group text to several women, they began appearing at his door. Each woman had a similar story about sexual threats and harassment from someone they should have been able to turn to for support. Each of them felt as deeply betrayed and disgusted as Niki did.

"So, did he finally believe you?"

She turned into her drive and pulled into the garage. "He had no choice. I had the proof."

"You still have it, right?"

"It's on my phone. I'm not about to turn that over to anyone except as evidence to the district attorney's office if they force my hand, and then only after I've downloaded the file to several different locations and devices."

Tex's grunt of disgust carried to her. "Smart girl, but it sickens me that you were forced into doing that. I wish I'd gone to pick you up now. I won't feel good about any of this until you're here, safe and sound."

"I'll be fine, Tex. It'll probably take me an hour or so to get everything together. I should be there by 6:30. I'll call when I get to the Sedtal's place." She ended the call and started gathering the ingredients and bakeware essentials she'd need to bring to the cabin. Once everything was set out on the cabinet she realized she didn't have any bags to transfer everything to Tex's place. Almost positive she'd seen a medium sized storage container sitting empty atop her pile of boxes in the shed, she went out to the patio to get one. She froze when she saw the door partly opened—no padlock hanging from the latch.

"Oh God. Not today, please!" Niki reached the shed in two steps and jerked the door open. She stood there, stunned and heartbroken at what she found, wondering what she'd done to deserve the day she'd had so far.

* * * *

Tex got out of his truck to pace a third time, anxious as hell to see Nik. He'd worked all day on the preparations, eventually satisfied that he'd set everything up the way he wanted. Finally the lights of her car appeared in the distance. As soon as he saw her face, tear-streaked and red-nosed from crying, he panicked.

He pulled open her door and she flew into his arms, obviously needing to be comforted. "What's happened?"

"I've been robbed!"

"What? No…"

"Yes! I was getting all my baking stuff together and went to the shed to find one of those empty storage containers. Everything's gone, Tex. They took everything—all of my mom's Christmas decorations! I have nothing left from her. Who would do such a thing? Who would steal storage containers full of Christmas decorations?"

He held her close, trying to sooth her, hating that she had to feel this way after the shit day she'd had at the office. "It'll be okay."

"It's not! I feel so stupid. If I'd just put up the decorations in my house they would have been safely inside." Her face crumpled pitifully. "I can't believe I'll never see it again. All the stuff my mom collected over the years. It's so unfair."

He placed both hands on her face and pressed a gentle kiss on her lips. "I may not know everything, but I know this for certain. You're about to feel a whole lot better. I hope you will, anyway." Now that he thought about it, he wondered if he'd made a mistake. He led Niki to his truck and deposited her into its warm interior.

"The container is in the back of my car. Don't forget anything," she sniffed.

He collected the storage container and slipped it into the bed of his truck. He checked on Niki's condition during the drive to his cabin. She still sniffed occasionally, but she had much improved since her arrival. As he approached the last bend in the road he stopped the truck and faced her. "Close your eyes for me, please."

"Why?" she said, her tone suspicious.

"Please?"

She gave him one last frown and closed her eyes. "You know I hate surprises."

"You'll like this one." He spent the last minute it took to get to his cabin reminding her to keep her eyes closed. By the fifth reminder, Niki's sharp comeback of "I will, dammit!" told him she'd surpassed her patience limit.

He parked his truck and turned off the ignition. "Hang on, I'm going around to get you, but don't—"

"Don't open my eyes—I know!" she snapped.

His chest rumbled with laughter as he opened her door and helped her to the ground. Tex adjusted her position for the optimal effect of his efforts.

"Open your eyes now," he whispered, and held his breath.

Her initial gasp of shock turned into pure delight as she clapped her hands together. "Oh, my God! It's just like the Riverwalk. Only it's better because it's so private. Oh Tex …" She turned and threw her arms around him. "I love it! This is the best surprise ever."

He'd worked for two solid days stringing thousands of clear and multi-colored lights on the cabin's exterior, including the deck, rails, and any tree within several yards of it. She'd asked to visit the San Antonio Riverwalk at night several times already, each time exclaiming in breathless awe at its beauty. Once the idea to create a smaller version of the spectacle of lights and water had taken hold, Tex knew he had to do it for Niki. "Hang on, that's not all." He ushered her several steps to one side so she could get a good view of the deck and pier all the way to the small wharf where she loved to sit and watch the water. Lights reflected off the glistening surface of the lake, multiplying the effects ten-fold. His heart swelled with pleasure at her delighted squeal.

"This is fantastic!" She faced him and stepped into his open arms. "You thought of everything, didn't you?"

He grinned, thrilled to put a smile back on her face. "I hope so." He led her toward the cabin, their hands clasped, fingers interlaced. As Tex unlocked his door he offered one last plea to the big guy for her not to be pissed at him, and led her inside. She stood still until he flipped the light switch—and Niki's audible gasp filled the room. Her mouth gaped as she performed a slow sweep of the cabin's kitchen and living room area.

"I can't believe you did this, Tex. *You* stole all my mom's Christmas decorations?"

His heart sank at the words and he braced himself for the worst. He couldn't tell by her tone if she was delighted or ready to scratch his eyes out for the tear-fest she'd suffered at his hands. "I'm sorry as hell for that, Nik. I never thought you'd go out there looking for a storage container. I hate that you drove the whole way over here as upset as you were." He faced her, his heart torn at the tears in her eyes, knowing he'd put them there. "Forgive me?"

* * * *

Niki stared into the depths of those baby-blues, stunned at his request. *Forgive him?* Could he possibly think she'd be upset about this? She shook her head. "Forgive you for what, Tex—putting a U.S. Marine-worthy-effort into pleasing your girlfriend? With everything you've been doing lately to help on this ranch, you took the time to recreate the Riverwalk with exterior lights. It must have taken you days. And then you went to the trouble of raiding my storage shed in order to fill

your cabin's interior with my mom's decorations."
She waved her arm at the open spaced area. He'd
set up a real tree next to the large windows, covered
it in the ornaments she'd grown up seeing on her
family's tree. He'd spread the contents of the
container throughout the room, going as far as
draping her mom's tacky multi-colored tinsel from
every doorway and frame that held still long enough
to get it. Every surface, nook or cranny of the rooms
held some memento from her mom's prized
possessions. The wood-burning fireplace popped
and crackled, sending a shower of sparks to the
brick hearth, adding to the cozy feel of the room.
She slipped her arms around his neck and lifted to
her toes to get eye to eye with him. "I am in awe of
you. And I am so unbelievably touched, because I
know you've done all of this for me."

He wrapped his arms around her waist and
squeezed, lifting her off the floor as their lips joined
in a kiss that she hoped conveyed so much more
than a simple 'thank you'. She wouldn't allow him
to pull away, but deepened the kiss, promising more
to come. He squeezed harder, and then slipped his
hands under her legs, taking her weight in his arms
and urging her to wrap her legs around his waist.

She broke from the kiss just long enough for a
murmured "Take me to bed."

The room filled with his rumble of laughter.
"Don't you want to see everything first? I worked

hard on all this." Despite his words, he reached the bedroom in a few long strides.

"Uh huh—I'm about to make you work even harder." She lowered her legs to the floor and dragged her palm down the front of his jeans. "Speaking of harder."

"I need you so bad it hurts, Nik," he groaned. "Seriously—it's been a long week without you here and I'm in physical pain."

She smiled. "Let's get this done, shall we?" No time for foreplay. In under a minute they'd torn each other's clothes off and fell onto the bed. Seconds later, he was buried inside her and pounding his way to a pleasurable release for both of them. She matched him, thrust for thrust until they both found what they needed.

They lay there afterwards, with his body covering half of hers, both spent and panting. She summoned the strength to look at him and smile. "Ooo-rah Marine . . ." A dimple appeared on the one visible cheek as his blue eye opened. Lord, she hoped to see that same blue in her children's eyes one day. Not that she'd dared to breathe the word marriage to him. Men like Tex may settle down with one woman—for a while anyway—but they surely didn't marry. She'd known that from day one. It had taken her until now to realize she didn't care. She loved him enough to take him any way she could get him for as long as she could have him in her life. With any luck at all he'd be a package-deal, baby included. Tex wasn't the type of man to abandon his child, so even if they didn't last as a couple, she knew he'd be a part of their lives.

"Thank you for all this, Tex. After the day I've had . . ." The day she'd had. It all came back to her in a sudden rush of disappointment and anger.

He moved to one side of her, propping an elbow on the mattress to support his head. "Tell me what happened. All of it."

She took a deep breath and gave him a play by play of her story, beginning from the second she'd stepped off the elevator. Tex was silent during her telling of the desk-assault, the tightness of his jaw a good indication of his level of anger. Even then, he kept quiet, letting her talk, keeping his opinions, his anger to himself.

He finally spoke when she'd finished, his tone pleading. "Please tell me that horrible woman is gone."

"Oh, she'll be gone. Or I'll release my recording to the press. A few of the women are considering pressing charges. One of them said B.L. had stalked her—that she still sent threatening emails. But she's smart, so they aren't obvious. The threats are just below the surface, you know what I mean?"

He nodded. "It's all about her getting off on the power of manipulation and mind games. That cold-hearted b—hmph!" He finished his comment with a grunt.

She laughed. "You can say it. She is a cold-hearted bitch."

Tex sat up quickly, his mouth set in a hard line. "But I can't, Niki. Because I'm a *man*, I can't say that. If your male supervisor would have done that to do, I'd be free to call him every name in the book, not to mention get him out on some back road and beat him to a bloody pulp. Nobody would bat an eyelash at that. But because your attacker was a woman, if anyone heard me saying anything about her, they'd jump on me for being a sexist pig. And let me tell you that I've served with plenty of females during my twenty years with the Corps. Every one of them earned the right to be called Marines—just like the men—hell some of them even more than the men. I treated each one of them with the utmost respect, because they earned it. I may have been a dog during my time served—"

"And after," she added.

He gave her a big nod. "And after," he agreed. "But I wasn't raised as a sexist. You've met my family. Do any of them seem like the type to let that kind of behavior slide?"

Niki pictured his parents, so loving and respectful of one another. She'd seen evidence of the same kind of relationship between Haley and Ben. "Definitely not."

"Right," he added. "That's why this incident frustrated the hell out of me from the beginning. It ate at me when you admitted you wouldn't have taken that from a male supervisor and would have reported him immediately. Sexism is defined as prejudice or discrimination based on sex. Your lack of immediate action against your female supervisor showed sexist behavior. The abuse of power is the same, no matter the person's sexual orientation."

"You're right," she said, finally able to see it from his view point. "It's like I told Betty Lou today, the fact that she's a woman hit me as an even bigger betrayal. But I shouldn't have had to put up with that behavior from anyone—man or woman." She leveled a look at him. "And I won't ever put up with it again."

"Amen to that." He leaned over and planted a kiss on her mouth. "Are you hungry?"

"Starving."

"There's still a little more to this surprise." He slapped her butt playfully. "Get cleaned up and I'll show you what I'm talking about."

She walked into the kitchen several minutes later, fully dressed and famished from their round of frantic, though satisfying lovemaking. She froze at the sight of the table, set for two with dishware bearing a heart-warming, familiar Christmas pattern. "My mom's Christmas china—she loved using it during the holidays."

Tex, ruggedly handsome in black jeans and a solid black shirt, pulled out a chair for her. She sat, taking note of his black boots, cleaned and polished, and pristine matching felt hat. No fair. She turned to putty in his hands when he went all 'Johnny Cash' on her. Once he'd settled her in her chair, Tex leaned over to lift the lid on a platter of barbequed ribs.

"Oh. My. Gosh. I don't even have to ask where they came from." She'd recognize the smell of that special sauce from her favorite barbeque place anywhere.

"Of course not." He chuckled. "You know I love seeing you make a piglet of yourself with these ribs." He opened a second container. "I even got extra sauce for you."

She stared, glassy eyed at the container filled with the rich, red-brown sauce. "I adore you."

He answered with another kiss.

She blinked when he stepped away. "What did I do to deserve you?"

"You gave me another chance, Babe. That's all I needed from you." He grinned and sat across from her at the small table, flanked by two red tapers burning in her mom's Christmas candle holders. "Dig in."

Nobody had to tell Niki twice to tear into one of her favorite foods. Ten minutes later, he stood and approached her side of the table, a self-satisfied grin stretched across his face. She eyed him suspiciously. "What are you up to?"

"Oh, about two sixty-five, but I'm all muscle."

She laughed at his answer, knowing darn well it was true. "Seriously, what do you have up your slee—" The sight of him taking a knee in front of her cut off the rest of her question. *No. Freaking. Way.*

He reached for something in his bulging shirt pocket. "Not quite up my sleeve, as you can see." He pulled out a black velvet box but didn't open it yet. "Nicole Elise Reeves … from the moment you entered my life, I haven't been the same. I didn't notice it at first, but you started to change me from that very first night we were together—transforming me into someone who could never again be satisfied with any other woman. I hate to admit it but it scared the living hell out of me and I ran."

He dipped his head momentarily before looking up at her again. "Eventually, I realized I couldn't outrun the feeling, so I stopped. At some point, I started running toward it. You make me a better man, Nik and I am undeniably, head over boots in love with you. I'd planned at first to do this at my folks place during Christmas dinner. Then I got to thinking it wouldn't be fair to put you on the spot like that. At least here, with just you and me, you have a chance to say no without being embarrassed."

Niki took a breath and held it as he finally opened the box, revealing a gorgeous square-cut diamond solitaire.

"Would you please agree to be my wife, Nicole?"

Niki's hand flew to her mouth. "Oh my God! Are you kidding me?"

"No. Is that an answer?"

"Yes! Of course. Of course I will!" Her left hand shook as he slipped the ring on her finger. She stared at it for several seconds before launching herself at him. Somehow, Tex managed to maintain his balance—kept them both from ending up in a heap on the floor. "I love you, Tex, I love you so much."

He hugged her tight, touched his forehead to hers. "I love you, Nicole. Now hold still for a second." He pulled out his phone and snapped a quick selfie of them.

Niki burst into laughter when she realized her mouth and face were smeared with sauce from the messy ribs. "You did that on purpose, didn't you?"

"You bet your ass I did. That one's for me." He reached for a napkin from the table and gently wiped the sauce from her face before snapping a second photo of them. "That one is for the rest of the world."

"I adore you." She kissed each of his eyelids, loving her big, strong, thoughtful Texas Marine.

"Good to know, but this isn't quite over with."

"What do you mean?" She rose to her feet and planted a hand over her heart. "I don't know if I can take much more."

"You'll love it … trust me." He straightened, draped a heavy quilt over her shoulders before leading her outside to the deck. He grabbed a power strip and pointed to a clearing just north of the cabin. "Watch that spot." He flipped the rocker switch to the on position and a large sign lit up with the words "SHE SAID YES!"

Niki laughed aloud as he took several snapshots of both her and the sign. "Who the heck is that for?"

His mouth twisted in that one-sided grin that told her to expect the unexpected. "You'll see." He looked to the north without another word.

"See what?"

"Wait for it, baby—just wait for it."

She looked to the northern sky and waited in silence. It took several more seconds for an explosion to echo through the cold, quiet December air of the Texas hill country. A split second after that, the northern sky lit up with a fabulous display of crackling fireworks. Open mouthed and utterly astounded at the thought of how much planning all this must have taken, she turned to him. "I can't believe you did all this." She laughed when he snapped a few more pictures of her. "Who's on the other end of those fireworks?"

"That would be a few of the ranch hands. They were more than happy to be a part of this." Tex wrapped one arm around her and took a few more shots of the two of them with the fireworks as a backdrop before putting his phone away. He slipped his arms around her, brushed his mouth against her ear. "You see those fireworks?"

"Mm-hmm," she purred.

"That's how I feel about you, Nik. I can promise I'll try my best to keep those fireworks in our marriage. I'll be here for you, baby—no matter what." He reached for a length of red tinsel looped over the deck rail.

Niki watched as he wrapped her mom's tinsel around them, binding them at their waists, finishing it off by draping it around her shoulders. "Tacky red tinsel and all?" She suspected he'd added this extra step for her—a symbolic gesture in honor of her mother, a woman he'd never had the honor of meeting.

He nodded. "I love you, Nik. Tinsel and all."

Epilogue

December 23rd

"Hey, babe—I've got something for you."

Niki stirred from her warm cocoon of blankets in the king size bed. She stretched her long legs and finally managed to crack open her eyes. Tex sat on the side of the bed holding a cup of steaming coffee—her favorite toasted hazelnut from the smell of it. Her boyfriend's thoughtfulness—scratch that—her *fiancé's* thoughtfulness astounded her. She remembered the previous night's activities and smiled. "Last night was unbelievable. I love you, Tex."

He leaned forward to give her a light kiss. "I adore you."

She pulled herself to a sitting position and reached for the mug decorated with reindeer. "What time is it?"

"Zero six-hundred hours and I've got a big day planned for us."

"You do, do you?" His dimpled grin shoved back any annoyance at being wakened at the butt-crack of dawn after such a long night. "It can't be any bigger than last night."

His careless shrug could have meant anything or nothing at all. After last night, she'd decided not to second guess this man's intentions. Whatever he set out to do, he did completely and with single-minded attention to the tiniest detail.

She cupped her mug in both hands and brought it to her lips, paused long enough to ask her question. "Are these plans of yours a carry-over of last night's big light-show finale?"

"Finale?" His boom of laughter reverberated in the room. "Honey, that wasn't the finale. That was just the beginning."

She managed to swallow the first sip of perfectly prepared coffee. "Okay, Tex. What do you have up your sleeve?" His tight grin, a sure sign of him holding back, piqued her curiosity.

"It depends on how you answer the next question."

She sat up straighter. "What question?"

"Last night you said you'd marry me."

She nodded. "I did."

"How do you feel about a Christmas wedding?"

"*This* Christmas?" His nod had her sucking in her breath. She released it in a rush. "But Christmas is only two days away. That's imposs—"

* * * *

"Nothing's impossible if we want it bad enough," Tex cut in. He leaned in for another kiss, this one designed to jump-start her sexual drive into full throttle. He knew what his lady liked. He pulled back after several seconds, ending with a soft kiss on her luscious lips. It would take a Marine Corp effort on his part to stay strong until he could bring his plans to final completion. "I want you as my wife as soon as possible. The question of the day is do you want the same thing?" Her eyes wide, cheeks flushed with desire, she gave him the answer he wanted.

"I do, Tex. I really do."

"Then I'm going to ask you to have a little faith in me. Do you trust me?" Her nod had him releasing another sigh of relief. He slapped her thigh lightly through the mound of covers. "Then get up and get dressed. We've got to be somewhere by zero eight-hundred. Casual attire is acceptable." He decided to wait and give her the details on the way to the city, praying she wouldn't get cold feet on the way to their destination.

They were in his truck by 7:00 a.m. He looked over at his beautiful fiancée, dressed in "I've registered us for an all-day pre-marriage counseling course."

"Are you serious?"

He chanced a glance in her direction as he nodded. "Totally." Her mouth gaped open as she stared at him—a sure sign of shock and awe if he ever saw one. "I didn't wait this long to ask someone to marry me without putting some thought into it, Nik. I want this to be my only marriage and I want it to last the rest of our lives. Are you up for it?"

She closed her mouth and swallowed. "I believe I am. And in case you're wondering, I want the same things."

He reached over the console and grabbed her hand. "That's exactly what I needed to hear."

* * * *

They strolled out of the building at 3:00 p.m., hands linked, their certification of completion tucked into the breast pocket of Tex's jacket.

Niki waited until he'd opened the door of his truck for her before raising a curious gaze at him. "What's next, oh great master of the impossible?"

He grinned as he helped her into his truck. "Next stop is the courthouse for a marriage license." He helped her up and walked around to climb into the driver's side.

"Oh my God," she murmured from beside him. "We're really doing this."

He grinned. "We really are."

"Are we getting married, like, *today*?"

He laughed at the panicked look in her eyes. "No. We have to wait three days after getting the license before we can tie the knot. We'll go to my folks place tonight, as planned. My dad's best friend is the Justice of the Peace. I'm sure he can be talked into shifting his schedule around to fit us in the day after Christmas."

"Oh, yeah, that makes sense," she said quietly, looking out the passenger window.

He reached across the console to take her hand. "What's wrong, Nik? Are you having regrets about not getting the big, fancy wedding you'd planned as a kid?"

She turned to him then, revealing eyes filled with tears. "I never imagined a big wedding. I'm more the small, intimate type. I never could see spending all that money on lavish receptions that cost enough to pay for a car. It's just—I always imagined my parents at my wedding, you know?"

He leaned across the console, took her face in both his hands and kissed her tenderly. "I know you did, sweetie. If I had it in my power to do that for you, I would."

The smile she sent him melted his heart, made him more determined than ever to make damn sure she'd never regret a single day of marriage to him.

* * * *

Christmas Eve

"Wake up, babe—I've got something for you."

Niki peered through the slit of one eye. "What time is it?"

"Zero eight-hundred and it's a beautiful day, sleepyhead."

She groaned, slightly hungover from a mixture of wine and their late night session of visiting with her future in-laws. "What is it with you and these early morning wake up calls? You aren't a Marine anymore."

"Sorry, but some habits are difficult to break. Once a Marine—"

"Always a Marine—yeah, seems I've heard that before. And don't ever let me hear you apologize for that." Niki looped her arms around his neck and pulled him close, burying her face into the crook of his neck. She breathed him in, loving her Marine. "What did you bring me?"

His chest rumbled with laughter as he extricated himself from her grasp. "Coffee, but you have to let me go if you want it."

"Mmm … okay." She pulled herself to a sitting position, adjusted her sleep shirt and finger combed her hair in an effort to look a little less rumpled.

He held out the cup and grinned at her. "It won't work."

She frowned. "I know. I'm a mess in the mornings."

"What I mean is nothing you do will ever make you more beautiful in my eyes than you are the first thing in the morning."

She took the coffee from him, took two sips and gave a satisfied grunt of approval. "Good coffee, and that's sweet of you to say, but I'm not sure I believe you. I know what I see my first glimpse into the mirror each day."

"Then you obviously don't see what I do." The bed sagged with his weight as he sat beside her.

She stared at him, still amazed at the difference between old Tex and the one she'd been close to this past six weeks. Sometimes it scared the hell out of her.

He reached out to touch her forehead with his thumb and forefinger. "Spit it out. What's going on in that head?"

She bit her lip, remembered what she'd learned at yesterday's counseling session about the importance of communication in a relationship. "Sometimes I wonder if I'm going to wake up one morning to 'pole dancer' Tex because you suddenly grew tired of me and our boring life." The smile he sent her went straight to her soul.

"Not a chance, baby. I spent enough years, months, days without you as I ever want to in this lifetime. You're stuck with me. Besides, who says it'll be boring?"

She reached out to stroke his face. He retaliated with a kiss to her palm before placing it on his heart. God, the man knew how to push her buttons in all the right ways. "So why have you woken me up at the butt crack of dawn, yet again?"

"I decided to give you your Christmas gift a little early."

She raised her ring finger. "You mean there's more to my Christmas gift than this gorgeous rock and the grand display back home?"

* * * *

Back home. The first time she'd called his place her home. Tex's chest tightened with emotion, surprised at how good it made him feel. "After everything you've been through at work, you deserve so much more."

"I'm intrigued. What is this mysterious gift?"

"I've booked an appointment for you at a spa salon in Orange in a couple of hours. You've got four hours of pampering ahead of you. While you're occupied with that, I've got a little shopping to do."

Niki clapped her hands, her eyes sparkling with pure delight. "Oh my God! I haven't had time for anything like that in forever!" She froze momentarily. "But your mom and I were going to spend all day breaking in her new oven with Christmas baking. It's too much to ask of her to do alone."

"There'll be plenty of time to get that done, and I'm picking up some things for her also. Besides, Haley and Ben are spending all day in Lake Erin with his family and won't be in until late tonight."

That brought a smile back to her face. She jumped out of bed, clearly pleased with her early gift and eager to start her day. She stopped suddenly and turned back to face him. "I want you to know something, Tex. I was terrified of facing this first Christmas without my parents. But, you've made it so wonderful for me and I will always—l-" She fell against him, obviously choked up, and wrapped her arms around his waist. "I will always love you for this."

He hugged her tight—grateful she couldn't see him blinking back tears brought on by her emotional confession. He'd known this would be a difficult holiday season for her—had vowed to help her get through it. Hopefully, after tonight, she'd look forward to each and every Christmas Eve.

* * * *

Niki turned in her seat again and eyed the few bags of groceries in the back seat of Tex's truck. "I thought you'd have done more shopping while I spent all morning in that spa."

Tex shrugged. "I got everything on mom's list. Seems like I had to go to several different stores to find what she needed, though. And the traffic was bumper to bumper. That's why I'm taking the back roads back to my folks' place." He reached over to take her hand. "Did you enjoy your spa session? You look relaxed."

She frowned. "I did, thank you—but, after all the time they spent on my hair, nails and makeup, I hope I look a little more than relaxed." She used one hand to wave at her flawlessly made-up face and hair—swept upward in a partial up-do that bared sections of her neck. "I realize it's a bit much for Christmas Eve at home with the family, but still . . ."

He laughed at her subtle dig, loving her reference to *his* family as 'the' family. He hoped it meant she already considered them her family, which she would be soon. Since Thanksgiving, his parents and sister had embraced her as one of their own.

"You're gorgeous, babe. But, my statement from this morning still stands. I love that you're happy with the results, but I still say you're sexiest first thing in the morning. In all fairness, maybe that's just because I love waking up to find you in my bed each day." Something he hoped to find every day for the rest of his life. He brought her hand to his lips and kissed the spot above her knuckles.

"What did I do to deserve you, Tex?"

He glanced in her direction, not terribly surprised to find her teary-eyed. Niki's tender-heartedness far surpassed her beauty in his mind. He'd seen her cry through everything from sappy Christmas movies, to Feed the World, St. Jude and SPCA commercials—and it always touched him enough to call in a donation. He answered honestly. "You took me back, Nik. After all my screw-ups— after my neglect—you gave me another chance. My goal hasn't changed. I plan to make sure you never regret it for a second."

"Well . . ." She sniffed loudly and used her right pinkie to wipe away her tears. "You're doing a damn good job of that."

They spent the several minutes it took to get back to his parents' place making small talk and listening to the local radio station. Tex relied on his training as a Marine to keep calm—even then struggled to settle his nerves when they arrived at their destination to find a red SUV parked in the drive.

Niki eyed the vehicle curiously. "Looks like your parents got some company while we were out. Were they expecting any family to come in?"

Tex grinned. "I guess there's only one way to find out." He threw his truck into park and turned off the ignition. This was about to get a whole lot more interesting. He looped most of the bags over his arm—let her grab a couple to keep things as normal as possible.

She started for the front door of the house, paused to read the plates of the new arrival. "Those are Missouri plates."

He nodded. "Yeah—they sure are." He waited until she headed for the door at a fast clip to call out. "Don't twist your ankle running in those boots."

He laughed when she threw open the door and entered the house. Seconds later, her squeals of excitement carried out to him. He entered the room to find her wrapped in Meagan's arms, the two of them jumping excitedly.

Niki stepped back from her old friend. "Oh my God, you're here! I can't believe it. We weren't expecting you until sometime tomorrow."

"I know," Meagan said, laughing. She sent a private look Tex's direction. "But something came up that we just couldn't pass up."

Niki glanced from Tex to Meagan, and then back to Tex. "What am I missing?"

Buck entered the room and threw himself at her at a dead run. "Aunt Nik! We dwove a long way to get hewe to see you and Tex. You're beautiful!"

She scooped him up into her arms, spinning around in a circle. "Buckaroo! I have missed you so much. And thank you so much for making the drive. If I may say so, you are looking pretty darn handsome yourself in your new black jeans and white dress shirt." She touched the black bow tie at his neck. "What's the occasion?"

He lowered his voice to a whisper. "It's a secwet."

Tex leaned forward to look down at the little boy. "Not anymore, Buck. Why don't you go ahead and do the honors."

Buck's little brow furrowed. "I don't know how to do that."

Everyone in the room laughed—almost everyone. A look of confusion plastered Niki's face.

Tex grinned. "Why don't you go ahead and tell Aunt Nik why you're here a day early."

Buck nodded, his face masked with determination. "We're here for youw wedding this afta-noon, Aunt Nik. Awe you excited? It's almost time."

Niki's green eyes grew huge. "Today? She spun around to face Tex. We're getting married today? I thought we had to wait three days after getting the license."

He pulled some papers from his breast pocket and waved them at her. "Not if we completed the pre-marriage counseling session, and we've got our certificate of completion right here. What do you say, Nik?" He got down on one knee in front of their best friends and his family. "I'll propose to you one time in front of everyone to make sure you know I want this. I love you, Nicole. Will you be my wife … today?"

Smiling and teary-eyed, she nodded. "You know I will. I love you."

He stood and took her face between his two hands, kissed her amidst a cacophony of clapping and whistling from the others until Meagan separated them.

"That's enough!" she said, her tone frantic. "Don't mess up her make-up. That shade of lipstick is perfect on her and I don't know if she has the replacement."

Niki lifted her purse in a jubilant gesture. "I know, right? I bought one."

"Great, now let's get you ready for your big day. The J.P. will be here in one hour for a three o'clock wedding."

* * * *

Niki followed Meagan and Haley into the master bedroom of the Broussard's home. She stopped in her tracks. "Oh, wait—I have to get my dress out of the guest room where I stayed last night." She'd insisted on sleeping in separate rooms out of respect for Angie and Ricky Broussard. It'd been difficult, considering how much she loved sharing the bed with her fiancé.

Haley grabbed her hand and pulled her toward the door of the walk-in closet. "Everything you need is right here. My brother has been busy shopping for more than baking supplies this morning." She opened the door, revealing a full-length garment bag hanging from a hook.

"What—are you kidding me?" Niki stepped forward and pulled the zipper all the way down. She straightened, took one deep breath, her heart pounding in her chest. before spreading the vinyl to reveal the wedding dress he'd chosen for her. "Oh. My. God."

"Is that a good oh my God, or a bad one—I can't tell yet," Haley whispered.

"I think it's a good one," Meagan murmured.

Niki reached out to touch the off white satin, its bodice sparkling with crystals. "It's a good one. Everything I've ever wanted in a wedding dress. Mermaid style, long sleeved lace, off the shoulders with a small train . . ." She dropped her arms, and released a sigh. "It's exactly what I would have chosen for myself." She turned to Meagan. "You went with him, didn't you?"

Meagan's smile was answer enough. "You don't think I'd have left that up to a guy, do you? After all these years, I know what my bestie wanted in a wedding gown."

"This is perfect."

Meagan nodded. "That's what I wanted to hear. Now let's get you ready for your big day. There's a man out there who's waited a couple of years for you."

* * * *

Tex stood back to take-in the results of his planning. While he and Niki had been gone all day, various members of his family had transformed his parents' back yard into a tasteful venue for a small, intimate Christmas wedding. The simple, square arch centering the back fence had been wrapped in greenery and poinsettias, and draped in some kind of filmy material.

A center aisle split the forty-eight evenly spaced chairs into two groups—six rows of four on each side—just enough to accommodate the guests who'd altered their Christmas Eve plans to attend. Most seats were occupied by aunts, uncles, and cousins of Tex. The rest held Niki's old co-workers and friends in the Lake Coburn area, all invited by Meagan.

Tex approached the arch and shook the hand of the Justice of the Peace, one of his dad's oldest friends. "Thanks for fitting us in, Mr. LeBlanc. I sure appreciate it."

The man smiled so wide his eyes disappeared. "Like I would have missed this—Matthew Broussard finally settling down with one woman— it's a Christmas miracle I had to witness for myself." He nudged Tex. "Your dad says she's as pretty as she is sweet. He and your mom like her a lot."

"Yes sir. I'm one lucky son-of-a-bitch, I admit it." He looked up as Mitch approached from the rear.

Mitch gave him a thumbs-up signal. "She should be coming out any second now. Megs said to start the music."

Tex signaled his cousin, Greg, seated off to the side. Greg stood and began playing the guitar version of Canon in D.

Tex stood between the JP and Mitch, waiting in agony for his bride. Finally, his father appeared at the end of the center aisle, with Niki's arm looped through his. He sucked in his breath at the first glimpse of her. "Sweet Jesus . . ."

* * * *

"Oh . . ." Niki breathed. "Everything is so beautiful," she whispered to her future father-in-law. I can't believe he did this."

Ricky Broussard chuckled from his spot beside her. "He had some help, ya know."

Niki looked up at him. "Yes sir, I realize that, and I do appreciate it." She stepped with him to the end of the aisle and faced the front looking for one man. "Oh my God . . . just look at him."

Ricky patted her arm and chuckled. "Yeah, he cleans up pretty good, don't he? Just like his ol' man."

Niki answered without taking her eyes off of Tex. "Yes sir, Mr. Ricky—he surely does. Thanks for those genes, by the way." Tex's attire was similar to his outfit for Meagan and Mitch's wedding—black jeans, paired with a black tuxedo jacket and white shirt, with the exception of a newly acquired black bow-tie.

Niki walked slowly toward him to the chords of a gorgeous guitar rendition of Canon in D. She had no idea who was seated in the audience, or who played the guitar. Her gaze fixed on Tex—drawn to the singular beacon in a sea of sights and sounds. They finally reached the front and Mr. Ricky handed her over to his son.

Tex grinned down at her, his dimple on full display. "Hey there, beautiful."

She couldn't have wiped the smile from her face if her life depended on it. "My heart is about to explode, Tex. I can't believe you pulled all this together."

"I had help. One of my aunts is in the wedding biz." He shrugged. "She had some connections." He took both her hands, his gaze growing serious. "I just didn't ever want you to look back on this day and wish it'd gone down differently. I don't want you to have regrets."

She shook her head and blinked back tears. "Never, Tex. It's perfect."

He leaned forward, touched his forehead to hers. "You ready to get this done, Nik?"

She gave him a quick peck on the lips. "I sure am."

He took her arm in his and they faced the front. The JP ceremony was short but sweet. Soon they were signing papers, with Meagan, Mitch, and Haley signing as witnesses.

The JP cleared his throat loudly and introduced them to the attendees as Mr. and Mrs. Matthew Broussard. He winked at Tex. "And you, young man, may kiss your bride."

"Yes sir!" He took Niki's face in his two large hands, his voice full of emotion. "I love you, Nik," he murmured just before he planted a toe-curling kiss on her lips.

"I love you," she said when he'd pulled back. She looped her arms over his neck and gave him another kiss. He finished by leaning her backward over his arm as the audience exploded in applause and whistles.

He straightened, laced his fingers through hers and grinned again. "You ready to start the rest of our lives together?"

She smiled at her new husband—her heart full of love for this man and the family who'd gone to such great lengths to make this day perfect for her. "I'm ready, Tex."

They turned toward the audience, her arm looped in his, both ready to start their new journey. From here on out they'd make new memories, new traditions, and hopefully add at least a couple of new members to this wonderful family of theirs.

If you've enjoyed this story, please consider
leaving a review on the platform of your choice.
Thank you so much and Merry Christmas!

About the Author

Award winning author, Lori Leger, adores writing stories set in southwest Louisiana, where good Cajun cooking, helping your neighbors, and saying 'y'all' is as normal as hurricanes, heat, and humidity. She has twelve full-length novels, and

 five short stories published in four series: La Fleur de Love, its spin-off, Halos & Horns, Seasons of Love, Prime of Love series, one stand-alone Christmas suspense published with The Wild Rose Press, with two more in production and if God is willing, more to come.

She's contributed to the Sweet & Savory Cookbook of Amazon Authors, published by Top Ten Press. Lori also has an article published in the non-fiction book Writing After Retirement: Tips From Retired Writers, published by Rowman and Littlefield Publishers, and edited and compiled by Carol Smallwood and Christine Redman-Waldeyer.

Her fourth novel in the Halos & Horns series, "One Year to Forever" won 2015 Romance Novel of Excellence award from InD'tale Review magazine.

Book List

LA FLEUR DE LOVE SERIES
Some Day Somebody (Book 1)
Last First Kiss (Book 2)
Hart's Desire (Book 2.5 – A Novella)
Brown Eyed Girl (Book 3)
Heaven in Your Eyes (Book 4)

HALOS & HORNS SERIES
Green Eyed Temptation (Book 1)
Sarah Smile (Book 2)
Meagan's Marine (Book 3)
One Year to Forever (Book 4)
Tinseled Up in TEXAS (Book 5)

PRIME OF LOVE SERIES
Running Out Of Rain (Book 1)
Hanging On To Hope (Book 2)
Settling For More (Book 3)

Full Circle Love
(Four short stories about one couple, Cat and Zach, taken from the Seasons of Love Anthology series)

Christmas 911 – Stand-alone Christmas suspense with **The Wild Rose Press**

Links:
Website and newsletter signup:
   http://www.lorileger.com
Social Media links:
   http://www/facebook/llegerauthor
   http://www.facebook/lorilegerauthor
   http://www.facebook/cajunflairpublishing
   https://twitter.com/LoriLegerAuthor
      (@LoriLegerAuthor)
   Instagram: lorilegerauthor
   http://cajunflair.wordpress.com

https://www.goodreads.com/author/show/5171074.
Lori_Leger